SAINT HELENA

AND THE TRUE CROSS

SAINT HELENA
AND THE TRUE CROSS

Written by Louis de Wohl

ILLUSTRATED BY BERNARD KRIGSTEIN

IGNATIUS PRESS   SAN FRANCISCO

Cover art by Christopher J. Pelicano
Cover design by Riz Boncan Marsella

Published in 2012 by Ignatius Press, San Francisco
ISBN 978-1-58617-598-6
Library of Congress Control Number 2011930700

Printed in Italy ∞

CONTENTS

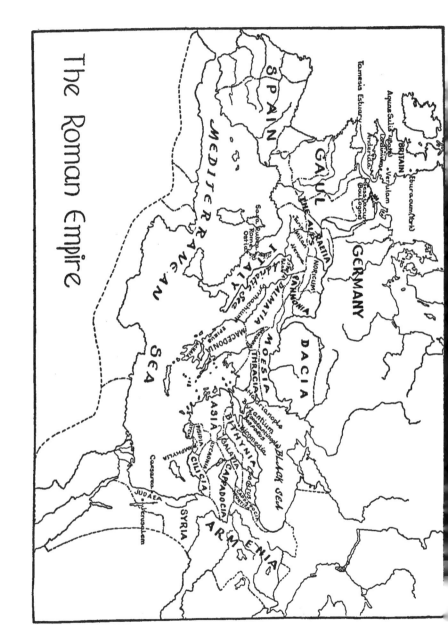

The Roman Empire

I

THE BURNING OF BRITAIN

PRINCESS HELENA stood on top of the chalk-white cliffs, watching a ship slowly vanish on the horizon.

The curly-haired thirteen-year-old boy at her side asked impatiently, "Mother, when is Father coming back?"

"I don't know, Constantine. It's a long way from Britain to Rome; it'll take weeks. Then he must talk to the emperor, and then he must travel all the way back here."

"The emperor has sent for him, hasn't he?"

"Yes."

"That means he needs Father." The boy smiled proudly.

"Quite right." Helena too smiled. The boy was growing more like Constantius every day—the same short nose and strong chin, the same firm outline of the eyebrows, almost straight. The same pride too, though there were people who held the opinion that the boy had inherited that from both his parents. . . . Well, perhaps he did.

She pressed her lips together. Pride was an essential thing. Without pride, no ambition. Without ambition, no high position in life. As a young girl she thought that it was something to have the King of the Trinovants as a father, to be a princess, and to have gray-bearded men bow to her with the respect due to her rank.

She used to think and speak with disdain of the Romans who thought they could rule Britain just because they had stationed a few legions here. She studied Roman history. Surely the Romans were no longer what they were when Gaius Julius Caesar landed on the shores of Britain. And she used to dream that one day she would unite the tribes and lead them against the Roman occupation forces.

But that was before she met the young Tribune Constantius, to whom all Britons were poor, ignorant barbarians and a princess of the Trinovants no more than an amusing novelty. They had clashed, inevitably; equally inevitably, they had fallen in love. Her father and Constantius' military superior had agreed to the marriage, both for exactly the same reasons: the security and peace of the island. And through Constantius she had learned to admire Rome, even to love it in her own peculiar way. For Rome, despite all signs of degeneration, was still ruling the world, and only Rome was the source of *real* power.

To Constantius, the gates of that power were wide open. He came from one of the oldest families of Rome. He even had imperial blood in his veins. And he was an excellent soldier. All his wife had to do was stimulate his ambition still further and give him a male heir.

Helena had done both. Less than a year after their marriage, Constantine was born. Six years later Constantius was promoted to the rank of legate, or general, and given command over the whole of Southern Britain. And now the new emperor, Maximian, had sent for him. This could mean—it very likely did mean—further promotion: the general command of another province, perhaps, or the supreme leadership in the Persian campaign. The possibilities ranged from Britain to Persia, from Germany to Egypt!

The night before he sailed, she had told him, "Accept whatever it is if it furthers your career. Don't think for one moment that I might feel homesick for Britain. Don't think of me at all. The only thing that matters is your career—your position, and that of our son."

Rome had two emperors now. Even the formidable Diocletian could no longer cope with the herculean task alone and had therefore raised Maximian to equal rank with himself. Maximian was a soldier. Well, so was Constantius . . .

The ship was gone.

Helena drew her cloak closer around her. "Let us go", she said, shivering a little.

They walked back to the road where the Centurion Favonius was waiting with the carriage. Marcus Favonius was a sturdy man with the arms and shoulders of a gladiator. He had made his way up from the ranks in the Twentieth Legion, and Constantine was delighted when his father chose that experienced fighter to be his trainer in military matters. Favonius had fought in Numidia and at the German frontier, he had won two silver discs for bravery, and he was the best man with sword and shield in the whole of Britain.

Helena liked the man because he was conscientious, reliable, and utterly loyal. "We're going home, Favonius", she said. "No, you take the reins this time. I'm a little tired."

"Very well, Domina."

A quarter of an hour later they were back at the villa, which had been the private residence of half a dozen Roman commanders of Southern Britain.

The day passed like every other day. The slaves were singing at their work in the garden. Constantine had his fencing lesson with Favonius. In the afternoon a little rain fell. One of the maids had to be punished for breaking a vase. The major-domo came to receive the list of invitations for the next week. There were fewer of them now, naturally. All official functions had been taken over by Tribune Valerius, the commander in charge until Constantius returned.

Helena sighed and then became angry with herself. This was the first day of many to come, of very many. She had always despised the clinging-vine type of officer's wife, fretting and nervous when her husband was away on duty. That was all that had happened. Constantius had been called away on duty, and it was not even dangerous duty.

Yet she had to force herself to be even-tempered with Constantine. She ate very little at dinner and retired early. When sleep would not come, she became angry with herself again. I *am* nervous, she thought, and I am fretting. What miserable creatures women are. . . .

When at long last she fell asleep, she dreamed that Constantius was being shipwrecked. He saved himself by clinging to a large piece of wood and landed on some island, where he was taken prisoner by soldiers in Roman uniforms. She remembered the dream when she woke up. Perhaps she ought to ask a druid whether it meant anything? No, she would not. Priests always saw an evil meaning in dreams, except when one paid them well.

At noon she saw the cloud. It was not an ordinary cloud, but a column of black smoke rising behind the hills in the direction of Anderida.

Something was burning there.

She stepped out onto the terrace to get a better view and found that there was a second column of smoke a little farther to the west.

Favonius came up from the garden.

"Look at that, Favonius. What do you make of it?"

The centurion looked, blinked, and looked again. "I don't like it much, Domina", he said slowly.

"What do you mean?"

"I don't know exactly, Domina, but it doesn't look good to me. Might be an idea to send a couple of messengers out—one up to the hills to have a closer look, and the other to Tribune Valerius."

"There is a third column forming", she exclaimed. "What can it be, Favonius? It looks as if half of Anderida is on fire."

"That", Favonius said, "is certain. But what started it? Just a moment, Domina. Say nothing. I think I can hear something . . ."

A few moments later, she too heard it; the clatter of hooves came from the road beyond the garden.

"Only one horse", Favonius said. "You won't have to send anybody, Domina. A messenger is approaching. There—it's an officer from headquarters."

The man stopped at the garden entrance and jumped off his horse. Helena went up to him. He was a young man, one of Valerius' aides, and he looked as pale as a ghost.

"What is it, Ausonius?" Helena asked, startled. The

young officer fought for breath. "Commander Valerius sends his respects, Domina," he gasped, "and would you please leave here at once and go inland? He suggests Verulam, but it might be better to go still farther north."

"But why? What has happened?"

"There is no time to lose, Domina. In one hour it may be too late; in two hours it will be for certain."

Helena raised her chin. "Pull yourself together, Ausonius", she said sharply. "What is all this about?"

"Anderida is being attacked by the enemy", the young man said in an unsteady voice.

"What enemy?" Favonius asked.

"We don't know. . . . They're dressed in Roman uniforms. They are three to one against us and there are more ships landing all the time. We shall have to withdraw. . . . The orders were given just when I rode off. I must go back, Domina. Forgive me. . . ." He saluted, turned, and ran back to his horse.

"Anderida attacked?" Helena repeated, incredulously.

Ausonius was riding off.

"I'll have the carriages ready in a few minutes", Favonius said. "You'd better collect your money and jewels, Domina, and clothes for the next few days."

"You really think we should . . ."

"Yes, Domina—and quickly."

"Then go and get my son first. Take him with you to the stables; make him sit beside you when you mount the carriage. I'll go and collect a few things. We shall need rugs and some food and . . . weapons."

Favonius grinned. "If you weren't the general's lady, Domina, I'd say you'd make a good soldier."

Half an hour later, two carriages were speeding north.

Looking out of the window of the first, Helena saw that the columns of smoke beyond the hills had combined to form one huge pall of blackness.

"What is burning there, Mother?" Constantine asked.

She pressed her lips together. She must not give in, she must not cry. "Britain", she said, tonelessly.

2

CONSTANTIUS IN ROME

LESS THAN ONE HOUR after his arrival in Milan,
young General Constantius appeared at the
imperial palace, accompanied by his trusted staff officer,
Tribune Curio.

The fat master of ceremonies walked up to them with
mincing steps.

"What is it you wish, General?"

"I wish to report to the emperor."

"Not today, surely? If you will follow me to the chancellery, I shall inscribe your name, and within two or three weeks you will be informed when the divine emperor will grant you an audience." He turned away and walked on. But after a few steps he became aware that he was walking on alone. Turning again, he saw that the two officers had not moved. "Follow me, *please*", he said, impatiently.

"Come back here", Constantius said sharply; and— somewhat to his own surprise—the master of ceremonies obeyed, although as a rule high-ranking officers meant very little to a man in *his* position.

Staff Officer Curio concealed a grin. He knew better than anybody that his chief had a way about him, and it gave him pleasure to see that he was not overawed by a gold-glittering courtier.

"I have come here all the way from Britain", Constantius snapped, "because the emperor has ordered me to. In his letter he says 'at once', and I obeyed. Are you going to obey him too, or are you not?"

The master of ceremonies stared at the pale young face with the burning black eyes, the thin mouth, and the energetic chin. Then he sniffed audibly and walked away.

Curio grinned openly. "You made yourself a new friend at court, I believe, sir."

"Can't see how the emperor can bear having him around, can you?" Constantius replied with disdain.

"Emperors", Curio stated, "are always unpredictable."

"Which means that I should be more cautious—is that it? I know your subtle ways of criticism."

"Well, sir . . ."

"Now, don't *you* start sulking. I know you mean well, and you know I almost always heed your judgment."

"Whenever you do heed it," Curio said, "I give a good, strong ram to the nearest temple of Mars. I've been with you all of five years, but it has cost me only two rams so far."

Constantius threw back his head and gave a short laugh. "As bad as that, is it? Never mind, Curio. The emperor too is a soldier, and soldiers always understand each other. By the cold nose of Cerberus, he's become emperor only because he is a soldier—and a good one at that."

"He should be", Curio assented. "That's why Diocletian chose him to be emperor together with him."

Constantius nodded. "Diocletian is a statesman, but no soldier. Maximian is a soldier, but no statesman. It would be an ideal combination, if it weren't for the fact that neither of them is of noble birth."

"My General . . ."

"Well, they aren't, are they? Diocletian is the son of an Illyrian slave, and Maximian the son of a peasant."

"You're forgetting that the walls have ears here", Curio muttered.

"I don't care if someone overhears it and reports it to Maximian. It wouldn't tell him anything he didn't know. Ah, here's our fat friend coming back."

The master of ceremonies approached. "I am charged to tell the general from Britain that he is permitted to join the dignitaries, notables, and officers in the main audience room", he drawled. "The divine emperor is at present having his noon meal."

The audience room was enormous and more than half-filled with a glittering assembly. The chief chamberlain, staff in hand, directed the newcomers to their places. Their steps were the only sound.

Suddenly the curtain at one end of the room was pushed aside with great vehemence, and a giant of a man appeared—bearded, bull-necked, and fierce, his face almost the same color as his purple tunic. He roared, "Where is the man from Britain? Where is Legate Constantius?"

"Here, my Emperor."

"Come in. All others will go."

The room behind the curtain was a small dining room. At least, the emperor had used it as that. Constantius saw that it was in a state of utter devastation. Somebody—it was not difficult to guess who—had swept a dozen or more dishes off the carefully laid oblong table. Roast pheasants, partridges, fish, figs, dates, fatty sauces, and multicolored cakes formed a horrible mess on the priceless carpet covering the floor. Instead of the dishes, a large military map was spread on the table. It was a map of Britain, as Constantius saw at once.

Beside the emperor a few high-ranking officers were standing around the table. Constantius recognized

Vatinius, the commander of three provinces in Gaul; Galerius, who was supposed to be one of the emperor's favorites; and Maxentius, Maximian's young son, as ambitious and ruthless as his father. They all seemed to look ill at ease.

"Constantius," Maximian said, suddenly quite softly, "you are the officer in command of southern Britain, aren't you?"

"Yes, my Emperor."

"Then what, may I ask, are you doing here in Milan?"

Constantius raised his eyebrows. "I am here on your orders, my Emperor."

Maximian's eyes narrowed. "I don't think you're mad," he said, "and I don't think you're drunk. You say I ordered you to come to Milan?"

Constantius drew a carefully rolled-up letter from his belt and gave it to the emperor without a single word.

Maximian glanced at it. "My hand-seal", he exclaimed. He read the few lines the letter contained. Then he looked up. "Who gave you this letter?" he asked hoarsely.

"The Tribune Allectus, one of Admiral Carausius' officers."

"Did it not strike you as strange that I should send you a message from Milan through an officer stationed in Gessiacum?"

"It did, my Emperor. Allectus told me that the messenger from Milan had fallen ill and that the admiral had given him the order to deliver it to me in his place.

He also put a ship at my disposal, the *Titan*. He said she was fast, but she took a very long time for the voyage to Ostia, and I began to suspect that something was not right. That is why I insisted on being received at once."

Maximian nodded. "I never wrote that letter", he said. "My signature is forged; the hand-seal is forged. I never sent you a message at all. You have been lured away from your command, and in the meantime Britain has been conquered by the enemy."

For one wild moment, Constantius had to control himself, so as not to ask the emperor whether *he* was either mad or drunk. True, he had felt that something was possibly not as it ought to be, but that was quite different from what he was being told now. Britain conquered by the enemy? What enemy? The Danes? The Franks? Nonsense. The man who had lured him away was a Roman officer himself, one of Admiral Carausius' men. Therefore . . . therefore it had to be Carausius. Carausius had rebelled. That sort of thing could happen only too easily when upstarts were occupying the throne. If the son of a slave and the son of a peasant could become emperors, the throne was within any man's reach, if only he had enough courage and enough armed men behind him . . .

"Carausius", Constantius said aloud.

"That's right." Maximian began to walk up and down the small room, kicking pheasants and fish out of his way right and left, and swearing under his breath.

"He must have struck at the Calends of last month", Constantius added.

Maximian turned around. "Right again. How did you know?"

"The tides were right for him then. That's the first thing to consider for anybody trying to invade Britain. He probably landed in Anderida"

"He did. Why?"

"Because Anderida is a good port but has no fortifications."

"Why not?"

"Because it was supposed to be protected by the fleet—by the very fleet which attacked it."

Maximian nodded. "Go on", he said. "What else do you think the confounded traitor did?"

"He probably sent part of his fleet up the estuary of the Tamesis and sent his cavalry into Londinium. The rest is easy enough."

"Easy, eh?" Maximian exploded with fury. "It's been your duty to see to it that it was impossible. What have you been doing all these years out there?"

"Protesting in vain against the systematic weakening of my forces", Constantius replied icily. "I had to send a whole legion to Gaul on Vatinius' request, and all of the troops under my command consisted of three thousand regulars and ten thousand auxiliaries of little fighting value. I have launched complaints eleven times in the last six years."

"I needed that legion against the rebellion in Gaul",

Vatinius said quickly. "I wouldn't have succeeded without it."

"One can't be strong everywhere", Galerius chimed in.

Young Maxentius said nothing. Instead, he was looking at his father from clear, intelligent eyes, full of curiosity to see how he was going to deal with the commander of southern Britain.

Maximian shrugged his huge shoulders. "Seems it hasn't been your fault", he growled reluctantly. "And Carausius seems to have a high opinion of your capabilities, or he wouldn't have taken so much trouble to get you safely out of the way. But the fact remains that Rome has lost a province . . ."

"The emperor will allow me to regain it, I hope", Constantius said firmly.

The faces of the officers around him were expressionless.

Maximian tugged at his beard. "Neither you nor anybody else is going to reconquer Britain within the next couple of hours", he said, not unkindly. "In the meantime, I'm hungry. How's that? Oh, yes—I upset the table when the messenger came with the confounded news." He clapped his hands, and a pale-faced butler appeared, trembling all over. "Another meal, Dromon. Not in this room, though. There's a curse on it, I think. Have it served in the Green Room. I want music too. —Maxentius!"

"Father?"

"Tell your sister and her ladies to join us at meal. And don't look so gloomy, all of you! I'll see to it that Britain will be Roman again soon enough. Stay with us, Constantius. You can do with a goblet of wine, too."

Constantius felt a little giddy. It was difficult to believe that he was not dreaming. Perhaps it was a dream, and he might wake up any moment now and find himself back on board the old *Titan*, rolling to and fro on her endless voyage. The arrival in Ostia; the fast ride north to Milan; the fat master of ceremonies; the roaring, raging emperor kicking away pheasants and fish; the news that Britain was conquered by a Roman admiral turned traitor; and now this sumptuous banquet in the Green Room—exquisite, elaborately prepared dishes, choice wines, and silvery feminine laughter . . .

Rome had lost a province, a province whose main part had been given into his charge—and here he was, reclining at the emperor's banquet table with an imperial princess lying next to him on the dining couch—the emperor's daughter or stepdaughter, he did not remember which. Princess Theodora—Theodora, the "present of the gods", or of a god.

The gods . . .

Many a time Constantius had wondered whether they existed, and if they did, whether they really took an interest in the affairs of men, except perhaps for some ironical amusement about man's strange ways. The philosophers never seemed to be able to make up their minds about it. —Well, if the gods existed and if they cared, they did not care much about Constantius. He had been a soldier all his life. He had climbed the ladder of promotion ambitiously, year after year, to become a legate at the age of thirty.

For six long years he had held the command of southern Britain without so much as the ghost of a chance for major action—nothing but small skirmishes with this tribe or that, punitive expeditions, that kind of thing. And then he had to fall for this stupid trap, that forged letter, and spend two months on an idiotic ship sailing at snail's speed around the Pillars of Hercules while the enemy attacked and conquered as they pleased . . .

Old Curio, who was still waiting for him somewhere in the palace, would probably call him lucky for having weathered the emperor's first bout of rage—and perhaps he was. But who was going to get the command of the re-conquest of Britain? And when would it take place? Carausius was an extremely capable man, both as an admiral and a general, and he was fighting for his life. This wasn't going to be easy. It would take some preparations—and if some other corner of the huge empire became troublesome, that would most likely be given priority. Britain, after all, was no more than an outpost of the empire, the uttermost western frontier, and an island to boot, which meant that trouble there would not spread automatically to other provinces. It would certainly take many months, and it might take years before action was taken . . .

Constantius passed a weary hand over his forehead and groaned.

A warm, dark voice beside him said, "I am sorry for you, Commander. This must have been a bad shock."

The princess.

He bowed his head to her. "You are most kind, Domina." He avoided looking at her. Perhaps she was just making sport of him. He knew only too well what Vatinius and the other officers would say about the commander who was not there when the attack started. And this was the daughter of a ruthless old soldier. Why should she feel sorry for him?

"You probably left all of your friends in Britain. Your wife, perhaps?"

"My wife—and my son." He had forced himself not to think of them. Why did she have to bring that up?

"Poor man", said the dark voice.

He looked at her after all. She was a beautiful young woman, and her eyes were moist.

"Tell me about them", she said softly.

He emptied his goblet of wine. "She too is a princess", he said in a somewhat unsteady voice. "Her name is Helena. She is as beautiful as she is proud . . . and she is very proud . . ." He broke off.

"Tell me more", Princess Theodora said. She had a lovely, winning smile.

3

THE ROMANS ARE COMING

H ELENA WAS SAYING: "The Romans are going to
come . . . The Romans are bound to come."

Constantine was standing with his back to her, looking out of the window. Children were playing in the
small, cobblestone street of Verulam. A patrol clanked
by at some distance—three men, as usual, never fewer

than three men. It was the only sign, perhaps, that the new masters of Britain still did not feel entirely secure.

The young man sighed. "Seven years", he said bitterly. "It's been seven years since Carausius landed, and you still believe that Rome is going to liberate us."

"Carausius is dead", Helena said quietly.

"Yes, murdered and replaced by his fellow mutineer, Allectus, the same man who lured Father away."

"We have no proof of that."

"It's clear enough to me all the same, Mother. I was a child when it happened. I am twenty now, and I have learned to think. What else is there to do but think, in the kind of life we're leading? Living in this provincial town in obscurity—in hiding, almost—afraid that any day now one of the tyrant's secret agents may find us out. Twenty years old, Mother, and I've never had the opportunity of doing anything useful! We have to live from selling your jewels, piece by piece . . ."

"True," Helena admitted calmly, "and there are only a few left."

"How can you be so quiet and so—so cheerful about it all, Mother? How can you still go on hoping that Rome will act? There was one attack five years ago, and Rome was beaten badly."

"The Roman commanded was Vatinius, not Constantius", Helena said.

"I know, Mother. But if Father was not given the command then, why should he ever get it?"

"He will get it."

Constantine shook his head. "You are amazing, Mother. I wish I had your faith in Rome and . . ."

"And in your father", Helena added. "You don't know him as I do, Son."

Constantine shrugged his shoulders. No good trying to convince her. Even staunch old Favonius was doubtful whether he would live to see Britain in Roman hands again. "I'll go and find Favonius", he said sullenly. "We'll fence a little, though by now I know most of his tricks." He grinned wryly. "I suppose it means that I know all of the tricks there are."

"Is old Athenodorus not coming today for your lesson?"

"I hope not. I'm sick of books, Mother. No one is ever going to make a philosopher out of me."

When the door closed behind her son, Helena sighed deeply. The endless waiting was bad enough for her. It was terrible for the boy, who could not see how he was ever going to shape his future. But it could not be long now. From time to time drops of news filtered through. Allectus was not Carausius. He was a tyrant like Carausius, but he did not have the dynamic strength of the man he had murdered to proclaim himself emperor of Britain in his stead. Also, Rome was not engaged in any major war: which meant that Rome could afford to think of Britain. Something was bound to happen.

She rose and went to her bedroom. Sitting down at her dressing table, she took up an oblong disc of polished silver and stared at herself. She was still beautiful, but

there was a network of tiny lines around her eyes—
around the corners of her mouth, too. As so often before, she felt a pang of bitterness and fear.

Come soon, Constantius, she thought, or you'll find I
have become an old woman. Come soon, husband.

The news came, sudden as a stroke of lightning and
spreading like wildfire: the Romans were coming.

Favonius was one of the first to pick it up—from a
Carausian officer who, on his way north, stopped at the
veteran's favorite inn and drank himself into a stupor.
Before the officer lost consciousness, Favonius managed
to get two bits of news out of him: that a huge Roman
fleet had been sighted approaching the southern coast,
and that the officer had been sent to Eburacum
to inform the garrison there and have it put on war-
footing. When the man was snoring, Favonius cold-
bloodedly stole the papers he carried and took them
home for his mistress to read.

Helena read. Then she shouted for Constantine. The
young man stared at her almost in awe. She seemed to
have grown taller; her eyes were blazing. "Your father is
in command", she said triumphantly.

"Mother! How can you know that?"

"It says so in this report."

"But . . . but how can the Carausians know? There
has been no landing yet, surely."

"No, but they have intelligence reports from Gaul,
from the town of Gessiacum."

Behind Constantine stood old Favonius, grinning all over his face. The young man said, beaming, "Looks as if you were right, Mother." But then he frowned. "Gessiacum", he muttered. "I've been thinking about it so often. That's the Carausian bridgehead across the channel. They never gave it up. They're keeping the main part of their fleet there, too. If that fleet makes a sortie now, father will be caught between it and the coastal fortifications . . ."

"Your father", Helena said, "has been thinking about that too. The report says he blockaded Gessiacum with his own fleet and had a giant mound of masonry built across the harbor. The Carausians could not get out, for they would have sailed right into your father's fleet, more powerful than their own. They had to stay in port and watch the mound growing until the harbor entrance was closed. Then your father attacked in force; Gessia-cum has fallen, and Constantius has seized all of the ships in port. They will take part in the landing under his command."

Constantine looked at Favonius. They grinned at each other. Then they began to dance, smacking their thighs and shouting with joy.

"Stop it", Helena ordered. "There is work to be done. We must pack everything. As soon as it's dark, we leave."

Favonius nodded. "Where to, Domina?"

"Home, of course—to our villa in the south. That's where my husband will have his headquarters. Where else? And he must find his wife and his son there and his house in good order. Get busy at once."

They found the villa empty. It had served as a summer residence to one of "Emperor" Carausius' newly created nobles, but the man had left it in a hurry. The few slaves still remaining prostrated themselves before Helena and her retinue—Constantine, Favonius, and four servants, all of them heavily armed—and begged to be allowed to stay.

Helena gave them a curt nod. "You are in my service from this moment", she said. "That is, in the service of Rome."

"Well done, Domina", Favonius whispered. "This is the first house in Britain that Rome has seized in this campaign, and it's most fitting that it's the former residence of the Roman general in command and that it's you who seized it."

She gave him a brief smile. Then she began giving orders right and left. She inspected the kitchen rooms, the cellar, the stables. She made the female slaves clean both the private and the reception rooms. She was everywhere, and nothing escaped her attention.

Favonius and Constantine alternated keeping watch from the roof. Two of the male servants guarded the entrance, and the other two had been sent by Favonius to watch the two main roads that the first Roman troops would be likely to use.

In the afternoon, Constantine yelled from his post,

"Smoke! Two columns—one in the east, one in the north."

Favonius was drinking a cup of wine in the courtyard. He wiped his mouth with the back of his hand and looked up. "How far away, young master?"

"Six miles, the one in the east; double as much in the north."

The centurion made a few swift calculations. "You'd better come down", he shouted. "I'll send one of the sentinels up in your place."

When Constantine appeared in the courtyard, Favonius said, "No news from the main roads. No fugitives either, so far. There is bound to be pretty heavy fighting in the coastal zone. The smoke in the east is coming from Anderida, of course, but the attack there may well be a feint. The general won't have a task as easy as that of the late Carausius, Hades keep him. Carausius managed a surprise, and that's half the victory. But the Carausians knew that the attack was coming. That means that they will defend the coastal zone."

Constantine stared at him. He was thinking hard. "They'll give us a battle on the coast, of course, because they'll be afraid that the native population will rebel once they know Roman troops are back on British soil. Also, the Carausians know we're at our best in a battle on firm land. It's the opposite with the Vikings, and that's why they were always trying to lure the Vikings inland and away from their ships. Right?"

"Right."

"But why, then, the letter you intercepted to the garrison in Eburacum? They couldn't come down to the coast quickly enough to join in the fighting. . . . I've got it! They wanted them to keep the population in check, and perhaps to form a second center in case the battle on the coast went wrong."

"Right again", Favonius nodded. "Fortunately, the general knows all this too."

"How do you know he does? —No, don't say anything. The second column of smoke, the one in the north. My father is cutting off the retreat of the coastal forces and stopping the formation of that second center. The smoke must be coming from the road to Londinium. It's twelve miles north."

Favonius pursed his lips. "I've trained a good many officers," he said, "but they don't come often the way you do. Not that it's all your own merit", he added quickly. "Your father is a first-class soldier, and so would your mother be, if the gods hadn't made her a woman. All the same, you're pretty good."

"Did I hear right?" Constantine blinked. "Words of praise—from you? You must be getting old."

They grinned at each other. Neither of them considered even for a moment the possibility that the Roman attack might be repulsed and the invaders hurled back to the ships.

But Favonius said, suddenly grave, "You still have a lot to learn."

"That sounds more like you", Constantine said cheerfully. "What is it I have to learn?"

"You were ready to give up, weren't you?"

Constantine flushed. "What do you mean?"

"You know very well what I mean", Favonius told him. "You no longer believed that Rome would come back here. You had given up hope. A soldier must never give up hope, and if he does he must still go on fighting. Your father never gave up. Nor did your mother."

"But you didn't feel so sure about it yourself lately", the young man said angrily.

"I'm only a centurion," Favonius replied quietly, "and I shall never be anything better than that. Your father is a general; your mother is of royal descent. You too will be a general one day, and the thing I'm talking about is the difference between the general who wins his battle and the one who loses it."

The steel in their eyes clashed. Suddenly Constantine smiled. "You're right, of course", he said, still a little grudgingly.

Favonius nodded. "Glad you can see it. It's a good sign. I think I'll go for a ride now and see what's going on."

"I'll come with you", Constantine said eagerly.

The old centurion shook his head. "Are you going to leave the protection of your mother to slaves?" he asked severely.

"Then let me go instead of you."

"Patience", Favonius said, "is a gift of the gods, they

say. I need it badly. We don't know what's going on, do we? I might run into a band of Carausians, a large band. If they get me, they've got an old war dog who isn't much good to anybody. If they get you, they've got a hostage. What do you think your father's going to say when they send him the message: withdraw to the ships or we'll kill your only son?"

"My father will know what to answer, I trust", Constantine said huffily.

"Why put such a choice before him?" Favonius shrugged. He marched off to the stable, and the young man was sensible enough to let him go.

A few minutes later, the old centurion galloped away. Constantine saw him take the road toward Anderida. When he told his mother about it, she frowned. "He should not have gone without my knowledge", she said stiffly. "I wouldn't have permitted it. The road may well be still occupied by the enemy. And your father will come here in any case. He needs no invitation. I wish you had stopped him."

Constantine was silent, torn between shame and pride—shame because, far from trying to stop Favonius, he had been eager to go himself, and now he knew how much she would have worried about him; pride because she apparently thought that he could have stopped the old centurion just by telling him to stay. Perhaps she too thought her son would be a general one day. And so he would be, and, what was more, he would be the kind of general who won his battle.

"The house is ready for him", Helena said, and the strong joy in her voice made him look at her. She had had little sleep within the last twenty-four hours, but she looked younger and very beautiful. She had changed into a dress of blue silk, her best dress, and for the first time in many years she was wearing jewelry—a necklace of dark blue stones, a bracelet of gold, and a golden ring with a single pearl. They were the last pieces, the only ones she had not sold. If Rome had waited for another year or two, they too would have gone.

"Father will be proud of you", Constantine said, a little hoarsely.

She smiled. She said nothing.

An hour passed, and then another, and nothing happened.

Just as Constantine thought "He won't come today", the guard on the rooftop shouted out that he could see troops approaching.

"It may be the enemy", Helena said in an unsteady voice. She was pale and her hands were trembling a little.

"Away from the gate, you two", Constantine shouted. "You up there, lie down. They mustn't see you." He turned to his mother. "If it's the enemy, they are retreating and not likely to come in, unless they see armed men here."

She nodded. But before she could say anything, the guard on the roof yelled, "They're Romans, Roman cavalry. I can see the standards."

Helena gave a sigh of relief. Her eyes began to sparkle.

"At last", Constantine said triumphantly. "Roman standards on British soil. Father must have won the battle of the beaches. He is fanning out. He . . ."

"Favonius is with them", the guard shouted. "He is with the officer in command."

Constantine roared up to the man, "Who is the officer in command? Who is he? What's his helmet like?"

"Gold helmet with black crest, master. Don't know the officer, master."

Black crest. A staff officer, then, a high-ranking one. Not Father. Not yet. Why did Mother look worried all of a sudden? Surely she could not believe that something had happened to Father? Only the barbarian chieftains still exposed themselves to actual fighting. Roman generals didn't—well, not often. He could hear the clatter of hooves now. Cavalry, Roman cavalry. No longer Carausian renegades with their hated new emblems. Today was the day when loyalty triumphed, loyalty and faith and justice, and Rome, which stood for all these.

The wild, exhilarating music of the hooves beating on the road, the Roman-built road, rose and suddenly changed its rhythm as armored men reined their horses and came to a halt at the gate of the house.

There was Favonius, jumping off his horse—no, gliding off it as if he were dead tired. It was not like him at all, and his face looked strange, too, pinched and wrinkled as if he had aged a dozen years. Had the battle gone wrong after all? Did they come to get Mother and him and take them to the ships?

The high-ranking officer, with the golden helmet and the black crest, did not look happy either. A legate with short, aquiline features . . . Who? . . . Of course . . . Curio, Father's aide-de-camp. He was a tribune in the old days, when he used to come to the house every day. Curio.

Curio dismounted and stepped forward. He saluted, and Helena's answer, a gracious smile, died away when she saw how grave and worried he looked.

"Domina Helena," he said, "I am bringing grave news. May we go inside?"

"My husband . . ." she said breathlessly.

"He is alive and well", Curio replied quickly.

She smiled again. "Nothing else matters, Curio. Speak up, man, speak here. What is it?"

"Domina Helena . . ."—the old soldier gulped. He made a great effort to control himself and succeeded. "You have been out of touch with world events for many years", he said. "Changes have taken place, very important changes. And, believe me, the very life of the empire depended upon them."

She nodded. She did not understand what he was driving at.

"Both our emperors," he went on, "Diocletian and Maximian, are old men. They felt the necessity to call up younger men to help them in their task, men on whom they could rely implicitly. They chose two such men and endowed them with the rank of caesar. Thus Galerius was to take over the Orient and Constantius the Occident, under the overlordship of the two emperors."

"Yes", Helena said. Constantius Caesar. He was one of the four most powerful men in the empire now. Only one other man held the same rank, only two a rank still higher than his. And these two were old and could no longer rely on their own strength. Constantius' dream, her dream, was very near fulfillment. But this was great news, wonderful news. Why did Curio look so unhappy? Why did he talk to her as if he had to report a calamity, a catastrophe?

"It was a unique event", Curio continued. He was breathing heavily. "Both emperors felt that such power could not be given to anyone, however reliable, unless he was bound to them in a very personal way. Therefore Caesar Galerius was asked to marry Emperor Diocletian's daughter, Princess Valeria, and for that purpose his former marriage was declared null and void by the chief priest of Jupiter. Caesar Constantius . . . " —He broke off when he saw Helena falter a little. But before he could step forward she drew herself up again.

Her lips were bloodless, her face was ashen, but her voice was steady.

"Go on, Legate Curio", she said.

"Caesar Constantius", Curio proceeded in a whisper, "was asked to marry Emperor Maximian's daughter, the Princess Theodora. The marriage of the two caesars took place on the same day."

"Yes", Helena said.

"There was no way of informing you, Domina, as you know", Curio said. "Britain was cut off from the rest of the empire. The caesar had an intelligence report that you were alive and well in Verulam. So he decided to make his headquarters here, in this house. He will be here soon . . . with the princess." He gave a heavy sigh. At long last he had finished with this most distressing task.

"Constantine", Helena said aloud.

"Here, Mother", the young man cried. He was trembling all over. His right hand, around the hilt of his sword, was white at the knuckles.

"I wish to leave at once", Helena said in a clear, firm voice.

"Yes, Mother." Constantine turned away. But before he could take a single step, he saw Favonius come up with two of the slaves. They were leading half a dozen horses between them.

Helena looked at the old soldier. "Loyalty is not dead everywhere", she said. "Is it, Legate Curio?"

The legate stifled a sob.

Favonius helped Helena to mount, then mounted himself, and with him, Constantine and the slaves.

Curio stepped back and saluted as the little cavalcade rode out.

After a while came from afar the call of trumpets. The caesar was coming with his princess.

4

THE SECRET OF SUFFERING

T HEY WERE BACK in Verulam, back in the old house
that had given them shelter during the reign of
Carausius and his successor. Nothing had changed there,
and yet it was poorer, mustier, and more forbidding than
before. Hope had gone out of it.

For weeks Helena would not see anybody, not even
Constantine. Twice a day, one of the two slaves she had

kept in the household brought her food. Sometimes she ate a little, sometimes nothing at all. She wore black like a widow, the slave reported in a whisper, and she was terribly pale. But she never cried.

Constantine's days passed slowly. Every day seemed to have far too many hours. When Favonius brought the news—picked up, as usual, in his favorite inn—that the rest of the Carausian forces had been routed and that the whole of Britain up to the great wall was in Roman hands again, his face lit up for one brief moment. Then he said sullenly, "Rome's hands are no longer clean."

"They never were", Favonius said with a shrug. "There isn't such a thing as clean history. No good fretting about that. All a soldier can do is try to keep his own hands clean. That is often not possible, either." He walked off. No point in asking the young master to have a fencing bout. He knew the answer he would get beforehand.

Unclean, Constantine thought. Rome is unclean. The whole cursed world was unclean. No wonder so many stoics preferred suicide to going on living in a world like that, a world where a husband could repay the love and loyalty of his wife by vilest treachery in order to satisfy his ambition. Constantine considered that he himself should not have come back to Verulam. He should have stayed on in the villa until the great Roman commander came with his new wife, so that he might repudiate him as a father, and tell him that he hated and despised him and everything he stood for.

If the Romans had thrown him into prison or killed him outright for this offense against the dignity of Caesar Constantius, well, so much the better. What good was it, going on living here without anything to do, without a future? One thing was certain: he would never accept anything from the caesar as long as he lived.

Now there was nothing he could do. If he had been alone, he could have left Britain, left the entire realm of this caesar to try to make his fortune somewhere in the East. But it was impossible to leave Mother now—even though she would not see him for the time being. She had lost enough; he could not add to her grief. Perhaps one day things would be different. Perhaps . . .

"May I speak to you, Domina?"

Helena looked up. Davus—the slave—a mild little man, ugly, but a good servant and loyal. Speak to her? Was there something wrong? What did it matter if there was, she thought. Everything was wrong. Perhaps Constantine . . .

"What is it, Davus?"

"You haven't touched your food again, Domina."

"I'm not hungry."

"It's not my station to talk to you, Domina, but if you could see your way to talk to Albanus, I'm sure he would be able to help you."

Albanus. Help her. Help her? The man must be mad.

"What do you mean, Davus? And who is Albanus?"

"He is a priest, Domina, a priest of my religion."

The chief priest of Jupiter had declared her marriage null and void. She was not asked. Null and void—all the years with Constantius—all her love—the fruit of her love—null and void.

"Priests . . ." Helena said. "I will have nothing to do with priests."

"He knows the secret of suffering, Domina", Davus said. "That's why I think . . ."

"Go", she snapped.

Davus slunk out.

The "secret of suffering". Such nonsense! What was secret about it? It was not hidden; it never had been. The world was full of it, full of blood and misery and the tears of the guilty and the innocent alike. And that was why all priests were humbugs, talkers of rubbish, trying to cheat anyone gullible by saying that they were particular favorites of this god (or that), and that they could placate the god's wrath and make things all nice and rosy for the generous giver. They would assume a mysterious air, as if they knew all about the world of gods and were in constant communication with them. They acted as though they themselves were almost gods.

Slaves, of course, *would* believe in that kind of thing, Helena thought. Perhaps that was the only consolation of a slave's life. She would *not* see a priest, whether he be a druid, a chief priest of Jupiter, or the servant of any other god or goddess.

Constantius had never believed in priest or god either. He had to comply with the usual things, of course—the morning and evening sacrifice to the Lares and Penates—for the sake of the servants; the thank-offerings in the temple of Jupiter on Foundation Day and on the anniversary of the emperor; the religious ceremony when one of his officers married—that kind of thing.

But that was no more than a pattern of formalities, a tradition. Possibly, too, it was a good example to give to the troops. It was always better when soldiers believed, not only in their general, but also in some sort of a god. One day they might no longer believe in their general. But they would still believe in the god, and that might well prevent them from killing the general. And what was true about generals was true even more about caesars and emperors.

Helena's father, old King Coel, had really believed in gods—yes, and in goddesses too. But they were no more than glorified symbols of the virtues of his people. The Trinovants were a warlike people, and their main god was a great warrior. They were a fertile people, and their goddess was a superwoman with an army of children. All the Trinovants were her children. Her father had loved his gods because they were part of the Trinovant life.

Most likely, the "gods" were no more than a human invention to comfort men when life became unbearable. The foolish could not see that if there *were* gods who cared at all about human beings, life would never be unbearable—and that there would be no need to run to them and ask them to remember their duty.

Helena gave a bitter laugh. It might be amusing to ask Davus whether his Albanus had an answer to that one. It might be more amusing still to ask Albanus himself

Davus, that impertinent little nobody, invited his Albanus to come in, although she had not asked him to do so. Her first reaction was to tell him to leave at once; he was not wanted here. But she could not help feeling that it would have been cowardly. Indeed, she had expressed the wish, *to herself*, to see him. No, she would see him and blast him in the presence of his pupil—or disciple or worshiper or whatever Davus was.

She felt a little disappointed when she saw him. There was nothing of the druid about him and nothing of the pompousness of the Roman priest. He looked very simple. Not stupid, simple. He was a man of sixty or thereabouts—with a broad forehead, a strong nose, and clear, unblinking eyes. His brown tunic was clean, but rather shabby. The hands were small for a man of his class, and very sensitive. Something of an artisan, she thought, a man who is accustomed to very precise work. It was almost a pity to attack and crush such a gentle creature. But there was no place for gentleness in the world.

"Davus tells me you know the secret of suffering, Albanus. Is that true?"

"Yes, Domina Helena."

She smiled sarcastically. "Well, what is it?"

"It is a Person, Domina Helena."

"Oh, so the secret is a person. Then, *who* is it, Albanus? You, perhaps?"

"I am no more than His humble servant", Albanus replied. "And I am nothing except through Him."

She sat down. Her fingers began to drum on the table beside her.

"Who is he, then?" she asked impatiently. "But then perhaps you are not allowed to say that. You are a priest, Davus tells me, and priests are always so fond of making mysteries of everything."

"He is Jesus Christ, the Son of God", Albanus replied calmly.

So that was it. The man was a Christian. She knew all about Christians. They were a small, insignificant sect originating somewhere in the East—in Judaea or Galilee, one of those outlandish places. Some people seemed to think that they were rivals of the Mithra-worshipers, but surely that was nonsense. There were Mithra temples everywhere, but so far she had not heard of even a single temple to this Christian god.

Christians were simple people, most of them poor, going in for some kind of oriental mysticism. They were definitely not popular with the government. There were rumors that they hated mankind, that they poisoned wells, and that they sacrificed the flesh and blood of a human being on their altars. In some provinces the government had ordered strong measures against them, ruling that they were not allowed to own land and could not be accepted in the civil service.

She seemed to remember that Constantius had mentioned them once or twice, but she could no longer recall what he had said about them. So: Albanus was a Christian.

She would have broken off the interview at once if it had not been for that strange matter of the "secret of suffering" being a "person". She said, "It's a Jewish sect, I hear. Why should you, a Briton, believe in a Jewish god—or in his son?"

"The Jews were the people chosen by God", Albanus explained patiently. "They were the first to carry the truth of the One God through the centuries. All other peoples believed in a multitude of gods, most of them no more than symbols of natural forces. The Jews were chosen also to bring forth the Christ, Who would save the world through His life and death . . ."

"But you just said that he was the son of your god!"

"And so He was. But all that was human about Him was of His mother, a Jewish virgin. He partook of our humanity so that we might partake of His Divinity."

"He doesn't seem to have been very successful", Helena jeered. "Or do you believe that all is well with the world now?"

"The world was lost", Albanus said. "But it is one thing to save a man from drowning and another to restore him to full health. The Christ is the remedy. But the patient must accept the remedy if he wishes to be healed. One thing is quite certain: there is no other remedy but the Christ, and there never will be."

Helena shrugged her shoulders.

"There are so many religions", she said. "Why say 'Christ', if you can say Mars or Diana or Isis?"

"Because all of the others are fables, symbols, and do not really exist", Albanus replied.

"Neither does your Christ", she interposed. "Surely he has been dead a long time? Why, there were Christians at the time of Tacitus and Suetonius . . ."

"He died two hundred sixty-one years ago", Albanus told her. "He was crucified . . . for you."

"For me?" she exclaimed, horrified and shocked. "What an absurd thing to say!"

"For you," Albanus repeated, "and for me and Davus; for your son, for the emperor, and for every one of his slaves; for the Germans over the Rhine, the Negroes in Africa, and the people in the countries beyond Persia and India; for all those who died before Him and all those still to come—and yet for every one of us alone. He was the great Sacrifice that reconciled God with mankind."

Albanus then said, "Have you ever seen anybody die by crucifixion, Domina Helena?"

She gave a shudder. "No."

"There is no more painful death." Albanus' voice sank to a mere whisper. "And just that death He would endure for our sake. And in dying He took on Himself all of the sins and crimes that had ever been committed or ever would be committed, so that they could be pardoned. In what other religion, Domina, did God descend on earth to take upon Himself a human life, human suffering, and the most terrible death?"

There was no answer to that.

"There is still suffering in the world", Helena said after a moment. "And as often as not, it is the innocent who suffer."

"No one could be more innocent than Christ Himself ", Albanus said. "And those who accept Him will no longer regard suffering as senseless or unjust. They will accept it as their share in the great Sacrifice, the way a soldier accepts a wound in the service of his country. And it is, as often as not, the courageous soldier who is wounded."

She no longer thought of attacking. She had to try to cover up her retreat. "If your god were powerful enough, he would know how to stop the suffering of the innocent at least", she said sullenly. "I will not even mention my own—but that my son should suffer . . ."

"We all suffer from the sins of our parents", Albanus said. "But do you mean that you are quite reconciled to your own suffering, Domina?" The strange, unblinking eyes were grave.

"I—I don't know", she said evasively. "In any case, you have no right to ask such a question."

"I will ask another, then", Albanus said. "Are you quite certain that you have done nothing to merit that which has happened to you?"

That was too much. She jumped to her feet. "How dare you! How dare you stand in judgment over me!"

"God forbid that I should try to judge you", Albanus said calmly. "The judgment is God's alone. But you should ask yourself whether or not you are entirely without blame, and in doing so you must be absolutely honest with yourself."

"You seem to have forgotten to whom you are speaking."

"I am speaking to a human being for whom Christ died on the cross and who therefore must be of infinite value. I am speaking to a great lady who by right should be the wife of Constantius Caesar—and who would be, if she and Constantius Caesar were Christians. For with us there is no divorce, because marriage is a partnership of God, man, and woman—a partnership of three, not of two."

Once more there was no answer to what the man said.

"The most difficult thing for us is to be honest with ourselves", Albanus continued evenly. "We all want to believe that our own motives are pure, good, and un-selfish. But are they really?"

"I told you, I am thinking of my son and his future", Helena said defiantly.

Albanus nodded. "So you did, Domina. And I will pray for him."

For one moment she almost said, "Pray for me too." But she caught herself in time and promptly became angry with herself. It was absurd; it was ridiculous. Be-sides, he would have concluded that she was thinking not only of her son but of herself, as well. The whole thing was no more than a trap to make her admit that.

"Do so", she said stiffly and gave him a little nod to indicate the end of the audience.

He made a swift gesture with his right hand, first vertical, then horizontal, and withdrew.

The room suddenly was very empty.

What a strange man. And what a strange, incredible belief. A god becoming man and taking man's suffering upon himself. If that could be true, it really would be the "secret of suffering" . . . But how could it be true? And: What kind of a magical sign was this, first vertical then horizontal? . . . A cross, a sign of suffering . . .

She shivered. (I have suffered enough, she thought bitterly. I want no part in that god of suffering.) Everything had been taken from her—her husband, her position, her fondest dreams of rising to supreme power at the side of a great man. She bit her lip. So she was not thinking only of Constantine. She was concerned with her own suffering as well. And when she was thinking of her son, was it not because she wanted to sun herself in his career, his rise? Selfish . . . unselfish . . .

This Albanus was a dangerous man. He was stirring up things she had never thought of. She must not see him again.

Ten days later, Favonius announced that Legate Curio had come and desired to speak to her.

She frowned. "Let him enter."

No good refusing to admit him. He was the caesar's right hand and among the high Roman officials in Britain. It was better to grant voluntarily what he could enforce if he wished.

She told him just that, and old Curio looked down his nose and murmured that he would never dream of enforcing his presence on her, although, as she probably guessed, he was here in an official capacity.

She frowned. "Very well. What is it that you have to tell me? Do I have to go into exile?"

"Of course not", Curio replied, shocked. "On the contrary, the caesar has asked me to convey his most respectful salutations and to ask you what he could do for you so that . . ."

"The only thing he can do for me is to spare me any further communications", she interposed icily.

"But surely you are going to accept . . ."

"I was married once to Constantius Chlorus, commander of southern Britain. He is dead. The caesar who has sent you I have never seen. It is not my habit to accept anything from strangers."

The old legate sighed. "I was afraid of that", he said sadly. "But there is one thing at least that you cannot refuse."

"Is there?" Helena's words cut like a whip.

"Yes, Domina. You cannot, you must not refuse. However great your pride, you must not stop your son from embarking on a career of his own."

"Albanus", Helena said breathlessly.

"What did you say, Domina?"

"N—nothing. I was thinking of . . . something else." Albanus. He had been praying for Constantine, and now . . . But this was foolishness, surely. Besides, this offer came from the caesar.

"My son feels about this exactly as I do", she said aloud. But her tone lacked conviction, and Curio smiled.

"I am sure of that", he said. "Fortunately, however, I have not come to ask him to serve under Caesar Constantius."

Helena gave a bitter laugh. "Of course not", she said. "*She* wouldn't like it—the caesar's wife, I mean. How stupid of me not to think of that at once."

"I am in the position, however," the old legate went on, "to offer him the rank of tribune in the army of Caesar Galerius. He would be one of the caesar's aides at his headquarters in Nicomedia."

The joy welling up in her was so strong that it hurt, and she had difficulty to keep up her proud composure. "This, I think, he can accept", she said, trying hard to keep her voice steady.

Curio was delighted.

Only then the thought came to her that she would have to part with Constantine for years.

Nicomedia was in Bithynia, at the eastern shore of the Mediterranean. It was thousands of miles off, twice as far away as Rome. It would be five years before he would get a furlough. So many things could happen in five years. She might die before he came back, or something could happen to him. She pressed her lips together. "When do you want him to leave?"

"By your permission," Curio said, "I'll take him with me at once."

She drew in her breath sharply. Then she bowed her head. "So be it."

"Domina," Curio said, "you are the most admirable woman I ever met. Shall we call the young man in?"

Constantine, at first very stiff and formal, lit up with joy when he was told that he would serve Caesar Galerius in the East. "Do I have your permission, Mother?"

"You do. Tell Favonius to help you pack your things."

The young man rushed out of the room, his eyes shining.

"Are you going east, too, then, Curio?" Helena asked.

"No, Domina. I take the young tribune only to Anderida, where he will embark with four other young officers. Just one more thing. You said you wouldn't accept anything from Caesar Constantius, and I respect your words, as, I am sure, the caesar himself will. But you also told me that you regarded him as dead. If that is so, you are his widow . . ."

"Curio!"

". . . and as such entitled to a pension to be paid by the state. The state will have to fulfill its obligations, and there at least you can't dispute me. It won't be much", he added hastily when he saw that she was going to protest. "The state is a bit of a miser. Please don't argue about it, Domina."

She looked at him wistfully. "I really believe you are a good friend, Curio."

"That's settled then", Curio said cheerfully. "And now, if you will permit, Domina, I shall take my leave. You will want to bid farewell to your son. I'll wait for him outside the house. I have my carriage there and some of my men."

He left. Only a few minutes later, Constantine came in. Helena embraced him. "You will do well", she said. "I know you will."

Only when he had gone did she permit herself to weep.

When she recovered, she let Davus come in. "Go and tell Albanus I would like him to come again", she said.

5

THE EDICT OF THE EMPEROR

W HEN THE LATEST EDICT of Emperor Diocletian
reached the British town of Eburacum in the
year 303, Caesar Constantius read it and swore. He
locked the document away very carefully and for a few
days left it at that, except for making a number of secret
inquiries. Then, quite suddenly, he gave orders that all

of the army officers, officials of the household, and heads of the administration were to assemble in the main hall.

No one knew what it was all about, but those who had the "feel" of the palace whispered that the news was not likely to be good; there seemed to be danger in the air.

When the caesar entered, he had with him Velleius, the protonotarius, so it seemed to have something to do with a new law.

Constantius, pale and gray-haired, acknowledged the salute of the assembly and sat down on his throne of gilded ebony. Everybody else remained standing.

"It is my duty", began the caesar, "to proclaim to you a new edict of our divine emperor, Diocletian, counter-signed by my colleague in the East, the Caesar Galerius. The Protonotarius Velleius will read it to you."

Old Velleius, bald-headed, and with the profile of a vulture, cleared his throat and in a monotonous voice began to read. The divine emperor (the full enumera-tion of his titles took a long time) complained bitterly about the activities of a certain religious sect that had been giving trouble to the Roman authorities and was causing grave upheavals in all parts of the empire. The emperor had deigned to put the entire problem before a council composed of some of the more distinguished persons in the military and civil departments of the state. The conclusions of the council were the basis of the present edict, which was to take effect immediately in all of the provinces.

The adherents of the sect in question, went on Velleius, called themselves "Christians" after their head, a Jewish criminal who had been duly executed under the glorious rule of the Emperor Tiberius. They were trying to undermine the state religion by pretending that all gods were false except their own. By their own god they meant the aforesaid executed criminal. They refused to worship the genius of the emperor and denied his divinity. Their leaders—or bishops, as they were called—made laws of their own and appointed magistrates of their own. They collected community treasures and used them for the propagation of their faith. This movement had to be suppressed before it could poison still more minds. Otherwise, it was to be feared that the Christians might spread disloyalty among the army and set up their own military force.

At this stage the majority of the assembly felt very much relieved. They now knew that the edict did not concern them, although most of them knew at least some people who were Christians.

Velleius droned on. The divine emperor, therefore, had decided that severe measures had to be taken against that sect, and he deigned to order that the bishops and elders belonging to it were to hand over all books and scriptures to the magistrates of the state. These magistrates were to be commanded under penalty of death to have the books burned in the public market places.

All property of the Christian Church was to be confiscated and sold, the proceeds to be delivered to the

imperial treasury. Such persons as persevered in the belief and activity of the sect were to be declared unfit to
hold office or to be employed by the state. Slaves adher-
ing to the Christian faith could not be freed. No Christian was allowed to go to a court of justice, except as an
accused person. All churches of the sect and all houses
used for the performing of their vile and horrible rites
were to be demolished.

"Given at our palace in Nicomedia," read Velleius,
"on the day of the Terminalia Festival in the year one
thousand and fifty-six of the foundation of Rome."

There was a pause. The caesar rose. "You have heard
the orders of our divine emperor", he said with a little
shrug. "My chancellery will send it on to all of the
magistrates in Britain. No one—I repeat: no one—is
permitted to take measures on his own. The matter must
be dealt with in an orderly fashion. Now, as far as you
are concerned, officers, officials, and servants of my
household, this is what I have to tell you. Until now I
haven't cared much about what you believed in and
what you did not. From now on I shall have to, it seems.
I know that some of you are Christians. You will have
two days to decide whether you wish to give up such
dangerous beliefs or not. All of you will come back here
in forty-eight hours. Then we shall have a test. Your fate
is in your own hands. That is all."

Abruptly he left the room. Some of the faces in the
assembly, which now dispersed slowly, were grave and
anxious; some even showed despair. But others were

smiling and content. Soon there would be promotions for a number of people, for in forty-eight hours a number of valuable posts would be vacant . . .

When the caesar's household gathered again two days later, the main hall was changed. Near the caesar's throne an altar had been erected, and on it was placed a bust of the emperor. Despite the art of the sculptor, Diocletian looked in marble as he looked in life: a shrewd, cunning, hard-faced peasant.

In front of the bust stood a small bowl held by a tripod, and a vessel with incense.

Caesar Constantius rose from his throne, stepped before the altar, and threw a few grains of incense into the bowl of heated coals held by the tripod. The smoke curled up into the impassive face of the crowned peasant.

Velleius followed his superior's example, as did the six bodyguards who stood behind the throne.

The caesar said sharply, "All those who profess the Christian faith will step forward."

A hush fell over the assembly. After a while, a number of men began to move through the throng: five, then twenty, and still they were coming.

"Stand on one side", the caesar ordered. He counted them very carefully. "There are more Christians here than that," he said, "and I know who they are. Their names are on the list in my hand. Shall I read it, or are you going to step forward on your own accord?"

Tribune Sarto raised his hand. "There are eighteen of us, Caesar, who are ready to give up a belief condemned by the emperor and his council."

The caesar looked at the list compiled by the intelligence people. He mentally added Sarto's group of eighteen to the number of Christians lined up before him. "Eighteen—that's right", he confirmed. "Let those men form a group of their own on the other side."

There was still another name on the list, not accounted for by either group, but he was not going to pursue the matter that far. The man was not present in the hall, anyway.

"Very well", he said aloud. "Now all those faithful to the state religion will sacrifice to the divine emperor. Step forward one by one. Velleius, note their names."

This activity took more than half an hour. When it was over, the caesar said, "Now the group around Tribune Sarto will sacrifice."

The eighteen men did so, and the caesar looked on impassively.

"Now the Christian group", he ordered.

An elderly officer stepped up as their speaker. "We can't do that, Caesar", he said in a low voice. "Christ has commanded us to render unto Caesar what is Caesar's and to God what is God's. We can die for the emperor, but we cannot worship him."

The caesar looked at them in silence. None of the men moved. From the entrance of the hall came the sound of steps. He looked up.

The Legate Curio walked across, gave a polite salute, and . . . joined the Christian group.

The caesar nodded thoughtfully. "Thank you, my friends", he said. "The test is over. Now, it seems to me that what the emperor really wanted to know was whether he could rely on the loyalty of his servants or not. That must be the spirit behind this edict. It seems to me also that one cannot very well rely on the loyalty of men who are ready to renounce their faith as soon as their position is in danger. Therefore, the group around Tribune Sarto is dismissed from my service forthwith."

The assembly all stared at him—dumbfounded, thunderstruck.

"These Christians here, on the other hand," the caesar went on, "have proved that they are ready to resist and to uphold their faith. Men like that do not have to sacrifice to the genius of the emperor. Their simple word is their bond. They will therefore retain their posts. The officers among them will be transferred to my bodyguard. I know that with them my life is as safe as the honor of the emperor. You may go, all of you, except for Legate Curio."

The elderly officer heading the Christian group spoke out suddenly, "Victory and long life to Caesar Constantius!" And the call was taken up by almost the entire assembly. The members of the group around Sarto were trying to get out of the hall without so much as looking at each other. Everyone else made room for them, as if they were unclean.

"You shouldn't have come here", Constantius told Curio. His tone was very gentle. "I deliberately didn't tell you about my little ceremony, and I knew you were still laid up after your attack of fever last week."

The old legate smiled. "You knew about my being a Christian, too. Your intelligence department seems to be working well."

"Come into my study", the caesar said. "We'll have a goblet of wine."

In the study, Curio said, "You yourself did well, too, if you'll permit me to say so."

The caesar laughed. "Diocletian will be furious, of course. But I'm Maximian's man, as you know, and my dear father-in-law doesn't care much about such matters. Besides, Nicomedia is very far away. Mind you, I shall have to carry out my orders."

Curio looked up, frowning. "Do you really believe that Christians are dangerous to the state?"

"I think Diocletian must have become a little mad. Most emperors do, after a while."

"*You* wouldn't", Curio said.

Constantius looked past him. "I'm Caesar", he said dryly. "It's a high rank, but not high enough to foresee what the future has in store. Let's leave it at that, shall we? Have some wine. And tell me, if you can, why a Curio, the descendant of some of the finest men Rome ever had—consuls and army leaders among them—should adopt the beliefs of a Jewish sect. I don't know very much about them, but I'm told they center on the person of one Jesus, whom they call the Christ, the "Anointed One", who lived a few centuries ago, came from simple stock, preached about some kind of a new kingdom, was arrested, tried, and crucified in or near Jerusalem. He is said to have performed all kinds of miracles, and Christians apparently believe that he rose from his tomb some days after his death."

Curio nodded. "A good summary of it. Except that He came from the lineage of King David. That's the oldest aristocracy in the world, Caesar. At the time of David, Rome was not yet thought of. But Jesus did live a simple life, and most of those around Him were poor people."

"You didn't answer my question. Why should you believe in him? You're not a Jew."

Curio began to smile. "Forgive me, Caesar, but that question, from one Roman to another, is just a little surprising. Have we Romans not adopted the cult of the Persian Mithra, the Egyptian Isis, the . . ."

"I concede the point", Constantius interrupted. "But, nevertheless, you're not the kind of man who should take easily to a foreign cult. They're fashions with us. And I have yet to find anybody who is willing to forego his station in the world, his rank, and maybe even his life, for the sake of fashion. There is nothing very fashionable about the Christian religion, is there?"

"Thank God for that", Curio replied dryly. "And thank you for your good opinion of me. I certainly never cared much about fashions or fads of any kind."

"Then, what is it?" Constantius asked impatiently. "There must be something about it that eludes me completely."

"It's the truth", Curio said simply. "That's why I believe in it."

"The truth! Friend, you aren't going to tell me that you believe in the miracles of your Christ, that you believe that he came to life again after his death? Because if you do . . ."

". . . you will lose your good opinion of me", Curio said cheerfully. "I shall have to take that risk. Yes, I believe it."

Constantius shrugged his shoulders. "Incomprehensible. Why, man, why do you believe in what is so obviously nonsense?"

"You are far too intelligent a man always to trust the obvious, Caesar", came the surprising reply. "Only dullards do, because they lack the necessary brains and imagination to see that every rule has its exceptions."

"True", Constantius admitted.

"Well, then, when an ordinary man dies, he does not come to life again—not in this world, at least. And an ordinary man cannot perform a miracle. But if a man should be God—God-made-man and walking on earth, the same God Who made the world and gave it its laws—why shouldn't He be able to be the exception? If an ordinary man is able to change life into death by the stroke of a sword, or by an edict condemning Christians, why should God not be able to change death into life?"

"God . . ." Constantius repeated. "Everything hinges on the question of whether your Christ was God. Once you believe that, all the rest will follow."

"That's right."

"But why should you believe that he was God—or a god?"

"I believe it because He said so Himself."

This time it was Constantius who smiled and frowned. "I say I am a god; therefore I must be one. What kind of logic is that?"

"The logic of the emperors who declare their own divinity", Curio replied. "Or do you mean to say that you yourself are in doubt about Diocletian's divinity or, worse still, that you deny it?"

Constantius shifted in his seat. "Confound you, man", he spluttered. "That's—that's an entirely different thing. Oh, very well, we're alone", and he lowered his voice. "Of course I don't believe in the old man's divinity. But I have to pretend to believe in it. It's the custom of the times. And if I were emperor myself, I'd abolish it." He grinned. "Just a moment, though. *You* said you believe in the divinity of your Christ because he *said* he was divine. Then why not believe in the emperor's divinity too—or anybody else's who says so?"

"Because I'm not a fool", said Curio. "Why does an emperor claim that he is divine? Because he hopes that he will be regarded as one set apart from ordinary human beings and that no one will rise against him—or because the great power he wields has gone to his head."

"Or for both reasons", Constantius said.

"Quite. Therefore, he is either a criminal for hood-winking people into such a belief in order to further his own ends—or he is a lunatic, and here again, many emperors managed to be both."

"Really, Curio . . ." Constantius shifted again.

"Caligula was both, wasn't he?" Curio asked. "And Nero? You see, when a man says he is God, there are only three possibilities: that he is a lunatic, that he is a criminal, or that he is telling the truth. That last possibility is most unlikely, I admit, but we must take it into account if we want to be logical. Nothing, after all, is impossible to an omnipotent God."

"Well?"

"I have studied the life of this Man whom the Jews called Yeshua, Jesus, and whom we call the Christ, and I have studied what He said. Friend, if that Man is a lunatic, I'd hate to be sane. He lived impeccably. His words were simple, straightforward, honest, and pure as spring water in the mountains; and yet they contain the deepest philosophy—and, what's more, a philosophy that works practically as soon as it is applied. And when He speaks of the Divine, you just know that it must be true and that it cannot be otherwise. Such a man is not a lunatic. And he cannot be a criminal, for there *is* no criminal without a motive. A criminal wants to get something for his crime, either wealth or power. Jesus never cared for wealth or power."

"Wealth—that's for petty criminals. But power?"

"The Jews wanted to make Him their king", Curio went on. "They offered Him the crown, an assembly of five thousand of them—but He withdrew. Later He said that His Kingdom was 'not of this world'. Therefore, you see, He wasn't a lunatic, and He wasn't a criminal. There remains only the third possibility, unlikely as it seemed at the beginning—that He really was what He said He was."

"There is a fourth possibility", Constantius said. "This Jesus or Christ of yours never told you all this himself, did he? You were told his story by somebody else, by others. Perhaps he never said that he was God. Perhaps that story was invented later, maybe by perfectly well-meaning people. You should know how a story becomes changed, and changed again, in the course of time!"

"Impossible in this case", Curio said with a shrug.

"Why?"

"Because Jesus was condemned by the Jewish priests for having said that He was God and the Son of God, and because His closest followers were tortured and executed for teaching that He was God and said Himself that He was God. You are supposed to have our Scriptures burned. Well, they contain copies of the letters of some of His disciples and four accounts of His life written by four different authors. Two of them were disciples of Jesus Himself! They heard Him say that He was God, they preached that He was God, and they died for their beliefs. I know very well that a man can die for a wrong belief . . . but he himself must hold the belief. Would you be ready to die for Jupiter? Or for Mars, or Venus?"

"I should doubt it." Constantius banished a thin smile. "And you, Curio? Would you be ready to die for your Jesus?"

"Yes, Caesar," Curio said evenly, "and so would all of those men you saw today, the men whose positions you upheld because you are just."

Constantius cleared his throat. "I've had reports that certain Christians refuse to serve in the army. A centurion named Marcellus threw his arms away and declared that he would serve Christ alone; and Maximilianus, a recruit, refused to be enrolled and to swear allegiance . . ."

"He didn't."

"How do you know?"

"I know of both the cases you mentioned. Marcellus and Maximilianus refused only what your Christian officers refused today, to commit blasphemy by giving the emperor honors due to God alone. A Christian can be a soldier. Christ detested violence, that's true. But He never condemned soldiering as such. On the contrary, He had words of high praise for a Roman officer, the commander of our little fort at Capernaum in Galilee. What Christ really hated was hypocrisy, a hardened heart, and vice. What He preached was love and justice."

"Justice . . ." Constantius hesitated. "You called *me* just, a moment ago. Well, I haven't always been just, in the past." And then: "Have you had any news lately from Constantine?" The caesar's voice was not quite steady.

"He is doing very well in the East", Curio said gently. "I have heard that he has the makings of a first-rate soldier."

"Justice . . ." Constantius repeated. "It can be very difficult to be just, Curio. Ah, well. I'd like to have this new edict handled with clemency. I'll give my instructions accordingly, but I can't be everywhere at the same time. And I can't ignore the matter altogether, for that would be something like rebellion against the emperor, and there are many people who'd see to it that the emperor is told just that. Therefore, don't ask me for a favor I could not grant. I know you'd like to . . ."

Curio nodded. "I told you: Christians are ready to die for Christ", he said gravely. "Now I'm afraid you will see it happen in Britain."

6

TO EBURACUM

A FEW SMALL OIL LAMPS were burning in the room, which was packed with people. Most of the people had been there when Helena entered with Davus and with Albanus, who had greeted them at the door. She was a well-known figure in Verulam by now, but no one seemed to be surprised at her coming. Most of the people here belonged to the poorer classes. However, she recognized the wife of a rich merchant in the Street of the Silversmiths and the owner of the shop where she used to buy her cosmetics. Something strange about them, she thought. What is it?

Perhaps it was that they all seemed to be so eagerly waiting for something or longing for something soon to come. They were waiting as people wait at the gates of the palace to hear a beloved king say that the war had come to an end, anxiously, and yet in a strange sort of triumph. And they all loved Albanus. They smiled at him; they touched his simple robe.

He is a natural leader, she thought. But she knew that was not all. She had felt it herself each time he had come to visit her, and he had visited her often in recent months. He never came unless she asked him to. And when he came, they had talked of things she had never thought of before, things difficult, almost impossible, to believe and yet so beautiful that one's very heart demanded that it should be so. More than once she had said, "I wish I could believe that", and each time Albanus answered, "Faith is a gift. Pray for it, and it will be given to you."

Yet her pride revolted again and again. How could she believe in a God who allowed himself to be crucified, who died the most shameful death, hanging between two criminals? "The Cross is my obstacle", she told Albanus, and he nodded. "It is the obstacle of most people. For we all dislike suffering. But think of this. In every religion but ours, a man can say to his God, 'You may be powerful and eternal and omniscient—but there is one thing I can do that you cannot do: I can suffer and die!' In ours alone, God Himself has suffered not only with us but for us, and by His bruises we are healed."

After a while he added, "The Cross is the Tree of Life. The ancient Egyptians knew about it, darkly, and so do the Germans who speak of *Yggdrasil*, the holy tree that holds up the world. No doubt God planted the seed of wisdom in them in times long past. How I wish I knew where it is . . ."

"What do you mean?"

"The Cross of our Lord", he told her, "has vanished. No one knows where it is. Yet the saying goes that the teaching of our Lord will encompass the Roman world only when it has been found again."

She had felt the most curious sensation at that moment. Her heart began to beat tumultuously. She could hear it beat like a wild gong, thundering and thundering until her very heartbeat seemed to fill the world. It was all over before she was fully aware of it. It had been like a chariot thundering by so quickly that one could catch only a glimpse of manes and tails and wheels as it vanished in a cloud of dust.

So far she had never prayed for faith. Why should she pray for it when she was not even sure that she wanted it? She had never before taken part in any Christian assembly, either.

Perhaps, she considered, she would not be here today if it had not been for that infamous edict. Last week

Roman soldiers had burned down the Christian assembly house at the Porta Londinia when some of the worshipers were in it. There was similar news from other towns. She was not a Christian—not yet. She had not received what they called baptism. But she had to admit to herself that she had become more than only curious, and now that it was risky to be a Christian she wished at least to share that risk. If these people had the courage to defy the edict, so had she.

When Davus had come to ask for permission to go to the assembly, she told him she was coming, too.

Davus looked at her, aghast. "It's dangerous, Domina. The edict . . ."

"To Hades with the edict", she snapped. "Where is the assembly this time?"

"At the house of Albanus, Domina. But . . ."

"You'll take me there, then. That is all."

So here she was. And now Albanus raised his hand, commanding silence, and traced the Sign of the Cross over himself. The community followed his example. Then the priest took up an old scroll and began to read.

"When Jesus saw how great was their number, he went up on the mountainside; there he sat down, and his disciples came about him. And he began speaking to them; this was the teaching he gave. Blessed are the poor in spirit; the kingdom of heaven is theirs. Blessed are the meek; they shall inherit the earth. Blessed are those who mourn; they shall be comforted. Blessed are those who hunger and thirst for justice; they shall have their fill.

Blessed are the merciful; they shall obtain mercy. Blessed are the clean of heart; they shall see God. Blessed are the peacemakers; they shall be counted the children of God. Blessed are those who suffer persecution in the cause of right; the kingdom of heaven is theirs. Blessed are you when men revile you and persecute you and speak all manner of evil against you falsely because of me. Be glad and lighthearted, for a rich reward awaits you in heaven; so it was they persecuted the prophets who went before you. You are the salt of the earth. . . ."

The doors of the assembly hall burst open, and the red glow of torches shone into the packed room.

"No one moves", bellowed a voice. Bare swords glittered in the entrance. A few women screamed.

"Extinguish the lamps", Albanus commanded aloud. The men next to the oil lamps obeyed at once. The soldiers could not stop them. The room was so full that they could not enter it, and their torches alone were not bright enough to disclose more than a pandemonium of terrified people.

A whisper was racing through the crowd. "Out by the side door." Davus passed it on to his mistress. Helena shook her head. "These people are in danger. I am not. They must go first. And that means you too. Go."

Davus looked up to her, and it seemed to her that he was smiling. "For the first time in my life I must disobey, Domina", he said. "I can't go without you."

Reluctantly she rose and, along with those around her, made her way toward the side door. It was a small one, but these people trickled out in such an orderly fashion that by now at least a third of the assembly had gone. She too got out with Davus, but she refused to run as the slave suggested.

"They won't find us", she said contemptuously. "It's pitch-dark here, and they can't be regular soldiers or they would have thought of surrounding the house in case there was a second door. The prefect must have armed his city clerks for this outrage." She stopped suddenly. "Albanus", she said. "What has happened to Albanus?"

"I don't know, Domina." Davus began to cough. "Smoke", he gasped. "They're burning the house, Domina. You can't go back now. . . . Domina . . ."

But she was going back, and Davus followed at her heel, thoroughly frightened. They could see flames now, small, flickering tongues of fire rising from the hall. There were screams too. The fire was spreading. She could see a dark mass of people surrounded by men in armor. As she and Davus approached, somebody shouted an order and the mass began to move away from them.

They're marching them off, she thought. To the town jail probably. If only they hadn't got hold of Albanus. They probably had, though. *He* was not a man who would leave before the other members of the community had left. What were they going to do with him?

"We're going home", she told Davus. "And tomorrow morning I'm going to see the city prefect."

Davus said nothing.

The city prefect was a fat, pimply little man, very courteous, very obliging. He had shifty eyes and a mean little
mouth. What could he do for the noble lady?

He became much less courteous when she inquired
about Albanus. His eyes narrowed. What was the interest
of the noble lady in that criminal? Oh . . . yes, he was a
criminal, the appointed leader of a horrible sect so dangerous to the state that the divine emperor had to launch
an edict specifically against them. He had been caught in
the middle of one of their blasphemous rites. It was the
duty of the city prefect to see to it that such elements
were stamped out at once. The man had been executed.

"He is . . . dead?" Helena asked tonelessly.

Yes, executed. The man was a Roman citizen, so he
had the right to be beheaded, and he was.

"Murder", Helena said between her teeth. "Cold-
blooded murder."

The city prefect drew in his breath. The noble lady,
he pointed out, was no doubt too disturbed to realize
that this was not the way to speak to the highest municipal authority here. She had no right to speak of murder.

"What else do you call it?" Helena snapped. "You've
had him killed a few hours after his arrest. How can he
have had a decent trial?"

A shade of embarrassment was showing in the fat,
pimply face.

The trial had to be a quick one. Surely the lady knew
that a revolt had taken place—yes, a revolt of part of the
population of the town. Embittered, no doubt, about

the crimes of these Christians, they had tried to storm the jail. They had set fire to part of it, and a number of prisoners had perished in the flames.

The city prefect went on. "This Albanus died a quick, clean death", he said. "You may imagine, noble lady, what his fate would have been if he had fallen into the hands of the people." He gave an eloquent shrug. "He would have been executed in any case", he went on, avoiding Helena's eyes. "He would not renounce his faith, nor would any of his followers—not even the women and the children."

"Women? Children?" Helena stared hard at the man. "Do you mean to say that you had children arrested too?" A terrible thought welled up. "Prefect! Women and children were in that jail the mob set on fire? And they burned them alive . . ."

The city prefect flushed a little. "Very regrettable, no doubt", he murmured. "Perhaps, if I had had more troops at my disposal, it could have been avoided. But then, they were Christians, noble lady, don't forget that. I'm told that Christians sacrifice a young child as part of their horrible practices and . . ."

"Lies!" Helena jumped to her feet. "Filthy lies to cover up the crimes committed against them!"

The fat man leaned forward. "You seem to have much sympathy for these people", he said slowly. "Perhaps you are a Christian yourself?"

"I'm not", Helena snapped. "But you're doing your very best to make me become one."

She swept out of the room. In the street, her small carriage was waiting for her. Old Favonius took the reins. "Home, Domina?"

"No", she said. "To Eburacum. The caesar's palace."

Favonius fairly goggled at her. If she had told him to drive straight to the lowest gate of Hades, he could not have been more surprised.

"To . . . the caesar's palace, Domina?"

"You heard what I said."

"But, Domina, that's a journey of at least three days." He had regained his control. "We ought to make due preparations for such a journey—bedding for you, Domina, and victuals, and money . . ."

"I have money with me", she said. "I hoped . . . I wanted to buy the freedom of Albanus. Albanus is dead, murdered. I shall use the money for the journey. We shall buy whatever we need on the way. Drive on, man, and go as fast as you can."

7

BLESSED ARE THE MEEK

A HUNDRED TIMES during that terrible ride, Helena wished she had not acted on impulse. Not because of the ordeal of the journey itself, bad as it was, with hour after hour creeping by as they went on, the carriage rolling, staggering, groaning. They stopped a few times, to change horses and take a hasty meal; staying at dirty inns where poor old Favonius had to sleep rolled up on her doorstep to make sure that no one attacked or robbed her. Her thoughts were the worst ordeal, and whenever she chased them away they came back like hungry wolves.

It was madness to go to Eburacum. She did not wish to see him again, ever. What would he think? Why, he would not even receive her, of course. *She* was with him, the emperor's daughter. They had children, too. Perhaps that woman would laugh at her, from some window of the palace, while she was waiting for an audience with the caesar.

She could not face it. What on earth made her do such an impossible thing?

But she could not forget Albanus—his gentle face as he was reading blessing after blessing from the scroll; Albanus, whom they had murdered. Never before had she met such goodness, such patience. Yes, patience . . . with her. When she had fumed and fretted and stormed against him and his strange God, he had remained calm and loving. A new kind of love it was. He wanted nothing for himself; the only thing that mattered to him was to serve his God, and that God had demanded that he should love everybody else as much as he loved himself. If all people fulfilled *that* demand . . .

Suddenly she felt the most violent contempt for her own pride. What did it matter if they would not receive her at the palace? What would it matter if that woman laughed at her? She had to go to the caesar. She owed it to the shadow of Albanus—to his "soul", as he would put it.

This dreadful, stupid, senseless persecution of innocent people had to stop. Nothing else mattered. She
smiled grimly at the thought that Albanus would have
approved of what she was doing because it was what he
used to call an "unselfish" action. Perhaps that's what it
was. But she felt that she could not live with herself any
longer unless she went to Eburacum.

Then she thought: Nonsense. There's nothing un-
selfish about it. I just won't have that sort of thing
happen to these people. I won't have it. And if that
motive is good enough for the Christian God, so be it.

The carriage arrived at the palace early in the afternoon.
Favonius had to help Helena to get out of the carriage.
But once out, she walked without his help and even with
apparent ease, although her body ached all over.

Favonius asked for the officer of the watch. The officer came, took one look at Helena, saluted, and asked
what he could do for her.

"I am Princess Helena", she said. "Go and inform the
chamberlain that I am here to see the caesar."

The officer saluted again, led them into a large waiting room, and vanished. Soon afterward the chamberlain, a fairly young man, appeared—very polite and most
embarrassed. If only the august princess had informed
them of her coming, he murmured, she could have been
given a reception in accordance with her rank. He was
more sorry than he could say. . . .

"Then don't say anything", Helena interrupted. "Has
the caesar been informed that I am here?"

The chamberlain was bowing and scraping again. Such a pity, such a terrible pity, but only an hour ago special envoys had arrived from Milan with news of the utmost gravity, affairs of the state. "I don't know myself what it is about, most noble Princess. The caesar is alone with the envoys and has given word that he is not to be disturbed under any circumstances."

"In that case," Helena said, "I shall wait here until these people have gone."

The chamberlain raised his hands in despair. "I have no idea how long it will take, august Princess. Would it not be better if I made suitable arrangements at the guest house? I could send a messenger at once, as soon as the caesar is free."

"I shall wait here", Helena told him energetically. "You don't know me, young man. You have my permission to withdraw."

The chamberlain bowed himself out, still murmuring apologetically.

Favonius grinned. "You've established a bridgehead, Domina", he said. "No one could have done better."

She wanted to give him a severe look. Instead she smiled. Old Favonius had acquired the right to speak freely.

She had to wait now. It was possible, of course, that the chamberlain had told her a pack of lies, that this was Constantius' polite way of telling her that he would not see her. It was possible; it was even probable. But there was at least a small chance that the man spoke the truth.

In any case she would wait. If Constantius wanted her to leave, let him say so. Perhaps the . . . "princess" would do it for him.

Helena bit her lip. I'll risk it, she thought. I'll risk even that.

When, about an hour later, the door opened, her heart missed a beat. She was sure it would be the princess.

But it was a man who entered, slowly and a little bent, an old man with unruly, iron-gray hair, and a heavily lined face with pouches under the eyes.

It was Constantius.

She had prepared every word she was going to tell him as soon as she had bowed to him, the caesar, the representative of the emperor. But she did not bow. And instead of her words of greeting she said, "You do look tired, Constantius. I hope you are not ill."

"I am not too well", he said. "Too much work, you know."

But that was not all; it could not be; he was ill and could not hide the fact.

"Let's sit down, shall we?" he said. "You too look tired. Ah well, I'll be sixty soon. That's a good enough reason, but why you . . . ?"

"I'm well over fifty myself," she broke in, with the ghost of a smile, "and I had a long journey."

"Twenty-two years", he said in a low voice.

She nodded. For twenty-two years they had not set eye on each other. No wonder he was changed. It was only in one's memory that people did not change. She banished the feeling of compassion.

"I have come to see you . . . officially", she said in a matter-of-fact tone. "I have come to see the caesar."

He smiled. "That's rather unfortunate, Helena. I'm no longer the caesar."

She looked at him closely. "What do you mean? What's happened?"

"Both Diocletian and Maximian have abdicated. Galerius and I are their successors."

"You . . . you are the emperor now?"

"Yes, Helena. And apart from the envoys from Milan and my private secretary, you are the first person to know about it."

He was the emperor. There had been a time when that was the greatest of her wishes. Constantius—emperor— and a British princess—she, the empress—at his side, ruling over the huge, far-flung empire together with him. He had always been an ambitious man, but she had done everything in her power to stimulate his ambition more and more. And now he had reached the goal . . .

"I wish you luck", she said breathlessly. Only then did her thoughts rush back to the reason for her visit. "This is good news for me too," she said. "Or rather, for what I wish to ask from you."

"And what is it that you ask, Helena?"

"To recall that infamous edict against the Christians. It's a horrible, murderous thing, and you must stop it at once."

"As impulsive as ever", he said with a sad little smile. "You haven't changed so much after all. Why are you so interested in them? You haven't become a Christian yourself by any chance? Like Curio?"

"No, I haven't, and I didn't know he had. But it doesn't surprise me much. He always was a decent man. Are you going to have him executed?"

"What nonsense! Why should I?"

"Well, the Christian priest Albanus was executed, the gentlest and most decent man I ever met. I'm sure he never did any harm to anybody in his life, poor old man." She told him the story of Albanus's arrest and death, of the burning of the jail, and the attitude of the city prefect. "Such things happen under your rule, Constantius. You can't tolerate that, can you? *Would* you?"

"Curio", Constantius said pensively, seeming to ignore her words. "You have given me an idea there. I've been wondering for some time what to do with him. I think I'll make him governor of Verulam."

She stared at him, bewildered. "But you said he was a Christian . . ."

"He is. And his first action in office will be a proclamation canceling the edict. You didn't think I liked it, did you? I was forced to proclaim it because old Diocletian insisted on it. But now that he has gone, I can make an end to this bit of stupidity. Curio may even succeed in repairing some of the damage it caused, though that won't bring your friend Albanus to life again. I never gave orders for such executions, needless to say, but I know that some officials thought I was too lenient. They took the law into their own hands, perhaps because they hoped to gain favor with Diocletian behind my back. I'll have that city prefect arrested and tried here in Eburacum. I won't let Curio himself do it; it would embarrass him."

"Thank you", Helena said. Her lips were twitching, and she needed all her self-control not to burst into tears.

"Why should you thank me?" he said with a little shrug. "What I am doing is in the best interests of the state. Happily it coincides with your wishes. But I do have good news for you, as well."

"More good news? I can't think of any—."

"Constantine has been decorated for bravery. He's done very well at the Parthian frontier. Galerius wants to make him a legate, but I have other plans for him."

She frowned. "I don't think he is going to accept any favors from you."

"I think he will accept this one. I want him to be my successor on the throne."

Helena paled, and her hand flew to her heart. "The throne?"

He nodded. "I'm an old man now, Helena, and my health is no longer what it used to be. I don't think I'll last very long . . ."

"Constantius!"

". . . and I must think of a successor."

"But . . . the empress . . ."

"Theodora is a good, simple woman, very much concerned with her own health. She hardly ever stays here in Eburacum. She prefers Aquae Sulis, where she takes the baths under the guidance of her physicians. She has no political interests whatever. Our marriage was arranged by her father, who insisted on it if I were to be given the command of the troops to reconquer Britain. I was a very ambitious man then—and I paid that price. Had I refused, Maximian would have regarded it as a sign of high treason, I think. I certainly would have been finished, both as a soldier and as a statesman."

He passed a weary hand over his forehead. "It was a shameful thing to do, nevertheless", he went on. "It was a crime toward you; it was a crime also toward Theodora, for I did not love her."

"But you have children . . ."

"Yes. Six of them. The oldest boy is eight. Am I going to make him caesar at such an age? Besides, none of the children is a ruler, believe me. Constantine is. He is bound to be. He is *your* son. And I need a ruler for Rome—a good one—not another monster on the throne like Caligula or Nero or Caracalla. He must be a soldier too, for sooner or later he will be up against Galerius. The system of having two emperors won't work in the long run. Therefore, either Galerius or Constantine will be the ruler of the empire. Galerius is the real "father" of that edict against the Christians. You may imagine what he will do when he has all the power in the world. I need Constantine. Will you help me?"

Her eyes were luminous. "I will."

"Good. Good. Wasn't that old Favonius whom I saw outside? It was? Very well. I hope you can spare him for a few months. I want to send him to Nicomedia with a message for our son and to come back with him."

"He will be delighted."

Constantius rose. "I must go now. And you must rest. They're arranging suitable accommodations for you at the guest house. But tonight I want you to be at the palace again. You must be present when the cancellation of that edict is proclaimed officially. Besides, I want my court to show due respect to the mother of the future emperor."

He bowed to her, smiling, and left, his steps now a little firmer than before.

Slowly Helena made her way toward the outer door, the one which led to where Favonius was waiting for her. She was walking on clouds. Deep in her mind and heart she could hear the voice of Albanus: "This comes because your love was stronger than your pride", and then, in that special tone he always adopted when he quoted the Christ, "Blessed are the meek; they shall inherit the earth."

8

FLAVIA JULIA HELENA AUGUSTA

S EVERAL MONTHS LATER, Favonius arrived in Nicomedia, at the quarters of Tribune Constantine, to
whom he delivered two letters and a heavy round belt.

Watching his former pupil reading the letters, he
grinned to himself. Strong as Hercules, he thought. Arm
and shoulder muscles perfect. Legs, too. And no super-
fluous flesh, despite imperial banquets and the like. Just
as well . . . in the circumstances.

Constantine went on reading. Except that his lips were pressed together very firmly, he showed no emotion. In the end he looked up.

"Do you know anything about the content of the letters?"

"Everything", Favonius said stolidly. "I had to learn them by heart, in case they were lost."

Constantine nodded. "I shall try to get official leave. It won't be easy. Emperor Galerius is not entirely a stupid man, and he may guess that the real reason for my leave is not a sudden outburst of filial love. I shall have to tackle him when he's drunk—not too drunk, mind you, but drunk enough to forget caution."

"We should go as soon as possible", Favonius said.

Constantine smiled. "The divine Emperor Galerius gets drunk every day. By tonight I shall know whether he gives me leave."

"And if he doesn't?" Favonius asked innocently.

Constantine's smile broadened. "Then—we shall have to deal with the fellows he'll send out to pursue us. That's the only difference."

Favonius was delighted.

The young man pointed to the leather belt on the table. "Money?"

"Gold pieces and a few small bags of jewels, master."

Constantine nodded. "We shall need them. I'm going to the palace. There's a banquet on tonight. Get everything in readiness. We'll ride tonight, whatever happens. I'll be back at midnight or a little later."

He was, and Favonius was ready for him with two fine horses—Spanish bred—and two bags of food each for rider and mount, along with simple, inconspicuous traveling clothes.

"I've got my leave," Constantine told him, "but it's a trap. Drunk as Galerius was, he could still think a little, and old Licinius whispered something about losing a good hostage. I pretended not to have heard it and stayed on for another hour or so. Saw Galerius getting hold of Chanarangesh. That's his tame Persian, head of the secret police. Fortunately, they think that I must go and get my pay tomorrow at the quaestor's office, so we should be safe until then. Are the slaves asleep?"

"They've been drinking with me", Favonius said. "You've got some empty jars in the slave quarters, and your slaves are snoring. None of them will be able to tell that Persian when we left."

"Excellent." Constantine took off his ceremonial clothes and put on the simple tunic and cloak Favonius held out to him. "Where's that belt? Thank you. Let's go."

They mounted.

"Where to?" Favonius asked. "We have the choice between—."

"We have no choice. They're going to watch the ports like lynxes. Byzantium first. Then overland all the way. Come."

The streets of Nicomedia were empty at this early hour, and the two rode like demons along the starlit roads. When they reached the Bosporus, they roused an old fisherman from his bed and made him ferry them over to the beach opposite, horses and all.

In Byzantium they found a few hours' sleep at the house of the freedman Perennis, whom Constantine knew as an old servant of his father; but first Constantine asked the man, "Domina Minervina? The boy?"

"Still in Dyrrhachium for the cure, Tribune."

"Very good. Send a messenger there. I want them to travel to Britain as soon as they can. Can't take them with me; it's too dangerous. They are to go to Eburacum, to the caesar's palace, and wait for me—unless I get there before them."

"It will be done, Tribune."

Constantine grinned at Favonius. "I've got a wife", he said, "and a strapping boy, Crispus. She wasn't feeling well after the birth of the boy, so I sent her to Dyrrhachium, where the climate is better. Just as well I did, isn't it. I wonder what Mother will say."

"The Domina", Favonius said, "will probably say, 'Why didn't you tell me?'"

Constantine shook with laughter. "So she will, you cunning old war dog, so she will. But if I'd told her about Minervina, she would have wanted us to marry in Britain. I'm sure of that. And I didn't want to go back— not then. They were just sending me to the Parthian frontier. Couldn't write from there. —Never mind. Soon we'll set all that right. I'm for bed." He stalked off.

Not tired at all, Favonius thought. And the way he

took in the news about his being the next emperor: didn't bat an eyelid. *If* we get through to Britain and *if* he becomes the emperor, the good old empire is due for something, and no mistake. Then he too went to bed.

The next morning they were off again, dressed as slaves and accompanying one of Perennis' caravans all the way to Hadrianople.

There they bought the best horses they could find, changed back into uniform, and rode off, up and down the hilly ways of Thracia.

Constantine was dreamy. After a while he told Favonius, "I like that city."

"City? —Watch your way, master, it's pretty steep down there. —What city? Hadrianople?"

"Byzantium, of course—what else? Did you see that it's built on seven hills, just like Rome? *And* it's a port city right at the frontier to Asia Minor and the East. It'll be a second Rome one day. But I shall have to give it better walls. Five of the seven forts are old-fashioned. Couldn't stand a regular siege for longer than a week."

Favonius grinned. "You're not the emperor yet, master, and you never will be if those fellows down there catch up with us."

Leaning back from the saddle, Constantine saw the glitter of armor snaking up the curved road. "You're right, that may be the enemy. How many do you think they are?"

"Thirty or so. Too many in any case. And our horses are tired."

"Clever of them to find us so quickly. Let's see who has the better horses."

After an hour or so they knew whose horses were better. Favonius' steed stopped, trembled violently, and then fell totally exhausted. Favonius swore.

"Stop it", Constantine said.

To the old soldier's bewilderment, he dismounted and put a handful of gold coins into the saddle bag of the stricken horse.

"Come with me", Constantine said. "Here, into those bushes. I'll tell you what we'll do. It's something the Parthian horsemen did to my detachment once, and I've been wanting to try it myself ever since."

They tried it. When the soldiers came up—a centurion with twenty-five men—they stopped, dismounted, and started milling around the two horses. Somebody shouted, "They can't be far now." Then they found the gold and at once started quarreling. The soldier who first discovered it wanted to keep it; the others insisted on a fair share for each. The centurion bellowed at them.

"*Now*", Constantine whispered to Favonius. They came out of the bushes like lightning, jumped on the nearest horses, and rode off. The pursuit was hot, of course, but the two managed to escape when darkness fell.

Still, the hunt was on now, and for the next week or so they never stayed longer than three hours at the same place, taking short rests in deserted barns, in caves, and later in the Dacian fields. Twice they had to ward off robbers. And once a peasant with his four slaves tried to steal the belt with the gold when they were asleep. But Favonius woke up in time, and the thieves got the worst of the short fight that ensued.

From Pannonia they crossed into Noricum, with its snow-capped mountains, less wild than those in Thracia but higher. The travelers had made good progress, but they were still in Galerius's Eastern Empire. The Roman commander in Noricum, Severus, sent one of his patrols to try to stop the fugitives but failed in the attempt.

"Galerius has sent them orders by sea", Constantine said, angry because Favonius had received a slight flesh wound in the left arm. "He commands the ports; it's easy for him. But I'll get even with him one day."

"All we have to do is to get into Gaul", Favonius said. "From there on we're as safe as in Britain."

"Because Gaul belongs to the Western Empire? That need not prevent Galerius from hiring a few assassins. — Ah! I have an idea. We'll get a few assassins of our own."

Favonius stared at him. "Meaning?"

"We'll hire a few dozen cutthroats and use them as our bodyguard. Then they can send us as many patrols as they like. We'll simply give them battle."

They found their cutthroats in Istria, where they were cheaply enlisted. It was just as well, for Severus continued his effort to get hold of them on their wild ride through the northern part of Italy toward Gaul.

After a day of sharp encounters, Constantine said,

"That's sixty-four horses we've lost since the day we set out."

"Not too many," Favonius replied with a shrug, "considering we shall soon have ridden across the entire length of the empire."

One day later, they crossed into Gaul, where the Roman commander gave them an escort of regular cavalry through the province to the port of Gessiacum, where a ship was waiting for them.

At Anderida, on the British coast, Constantine received a letter from his mother. The emperor was very ill. His heart was giving out. The shadow of death was approaching.

That very night, the emperor had another heart attack, the third within four weeks, and it left him weak and dizzy. Chrysaphios, the chief physician, shrugged his shoulders when Helena asked him, in a whisper, whether the patient would recover. "He may live for a few more days", he replied sadly; "he may go at any minute. I have done everything that can be done."

Helena turned away and sat down again, at the foot end of the low couch with the purple cushions. Constantius had changed almost beyond recognition. His face was the color of old parchment, the eyes and cheeks had sunken in. A few wisps of gray hair stretched pathetically across the balding head. The lips were colorless but for a bluish sheen. Was he asleep? His breathing seemed to be a little more regular, so perhaps he was.

But suddenly she heard him say, almost without moving his lips: "Constantine . . . Constantine . . ."

"He must be almost here", she said. She took a deep breath. "But don't you think you ought to have her . . . the empress . . . summoned, and the children?"

He frowned. "No." He spoke with surprising strength. After a while he asked for something to eat, and servants gave him bread and wine and a little porridge in warm milk.

An aide appeared at the door. Looking at Helena, he gave a slight nod, and she walked toward him on tiptoe. "The tribune has arrived, Domina", the man said in a low voice. Her face, thin and waxen from long vigils, brightened. "Quick, lead me to him." It was no longer strange either to her or to the palace staff that she was in virtual command here, despite the fact that she was still staying at the guest house.

She did not have to go far. As she reached the main staircase, Constantine rushed up to them, with Favonius at his heel. "Mother!"

She gave herself only the time of three heartbeats to embrace the tall, powerfully built warrior who was her son. "Come with me", she said then, disengaging herself. "He is awaiting you."

"I'm in time, then. Good." He looked very grave and . . . hard.

"Be kind to him", she said. "I never knew a man could change so much. And . . . the end is very near."

Constantine nodded.

"I must prepare him first", she warned. "Wait here. I shall call you." She slipped back into the sickroom.

The emperor had finished eating. He was looking at her, expectantly.

"He is here", Helena said. She had wanted to prepare him gradually, but these three words were all she could utter.

The emperor's sunken eyes began to glow, and he made a move to sit up. At once she was at his side, helping him, rearranging the cushions.

"Never mind that", he said impatiently. "Let him come in."

When the young man entered, the emperor stared at him as if he were having a vision. He thought: It is I, as I was in my youth.

Constantine thought: I have hated him all these years. I should hate him now, but there is nothing left for hatred.

There was a pause. Then the emperor said, "Injustice can never become justice. What has been done cannot be undone. For what I did in the past, I asked your mother's forgiveness . . . and she gave it to me. I am now asking for your forgiveness, too." And he bowed his head.

Something broke in the young man, and he fell on his knees beside the bed. The emperor's thin fingers touched his head. "I wish to be alone with . . . my son", he said.

When Helena and Chrysaphios had left the room, he said, "Get up, Son."

Constantine obeyed. His eyes were moist. The emperor looked at the picture of strength and youth before him. He smiled. "Was Galerius fool enough to let you go, or did you have to flee? Report, Tribune Constantine."

Constantine reported, and the emperor listened attentively, occasionally interjecting a shrewd question. Strangely enough, the long report seemed to increase his strength.

When Constantine had finished, the emperor said slowly, "You have done well. Now listen to me. I am dying. You will be the emperor, perhaps tomorrow, perhaps . . . even . . . today. When you are emperor, what will you do?"

"Increase your twelve legions to fifteen", was the quick answer.

The emperor nodded. "How long will that take?"

"To have them fully trained, at least three years. That means I must keep the peace that long, and I think I can. Galerius won't like it, but he won't find it easy to attack me here. By land his communications are too stretched, and by sea he is not strong enough."

Again the emperor nodded. "Within three years the political situation may have changed, too", he said. "Watch . . . Maximian. Diocletian is older and may die soon. If he does . . . Maximian may wish to regain . . . the throne."

"There should be only one emperor", Constantine said stiffly.

The emperor smiled. "Never say that again . . . before you are ready."

"I won't . . . Father."

"Now call your mother back. I want her to hear what I have to tell you. And tell the aide to summon . . . the legates and . . . prefects . . . in the anteroom . . . at once."

When Helena stood again at his bedside, he said, "You will be with him and . . . watch over him. That means . . . he will be safe." Then to Constantine: "You will rule. I entrust you with . . . the fate . . . of my younger children. I bless you for everything . . . you will do for them . . . and Empress Theodora. Yours is . . . the responsibility."

Constantine bowed deeply.

The emperor asked for wine. When he had taken a few sips, he put the goblet down. "My officers . . .", he said.

Helena passed on his order. The huge curtain was drawn back, and a multitude of high-ranking commanders stepped forward, clanking with swords and armor.

"Friends," the emperor said, "I am leaving you. It is my wish . . . that the finest soldiers . . . of Rome . . . should not be ruled . . . by the sovereign . . . of Asia. Before you stands . . . my son and . . . successor. You will find . . . Constantine . . . worthy not only of . . . his father, but also of his mother . . . Flavia Julia Helena . . . Augusta."

The murmur of assent of many voices seemed to give the dying man fresh strength.

"With the assistance of . . . the godhead . . . my son will also . . . wipe away the tears . . . of the Christians . . . and make an end to the tyranny . . . practiced . . . against them."

Helena fell on her knees, tears streaming down her face. "Thank you," she sobbed, "oh, thank you."

The emperor took a deep breath. Once more he spoke. "In this . . . above all . . . do I place . . . my hope of . . . felicity." A sudden shudder went through the emaciated body under the silken rug. The emperor's head fell back into the cushions. Chrysaphios rushed toward him. But all was over before he reached him, and the only thing he could do was to close the dead man's eyes.

Helena remained on her knees, praying.

Constantine stood immobile, the statue of a hard-faced young war-god. Then, slowly, he turned toward the commanders and looked at them, at every one of them in turn. If he was to fulfill his thought that there should be only one emperor, these men were to be his instruments. He looked at them, unblinking, testing, weighing their strength. Tomorrow they and the troops at Eburacum would have to swear allegiance to him.

There was triumph in his eyes.

9

MARCHING TO WAR

A LONG, SCALY SNAKE was seen crawling across the mountains, and the rays of the sinking sun made it glitter. From time to time, its head vanished behind clumps of trees, but it soon emerged again—for trees had become scarce at that height. On both sides of the snake the mountains rose two and three thousand feet above, some of them capped by eternal snow. The Alps.

Only once before had the Alps seen that kind of snake, more than five hundred years earlier, when the great Hannibal had crossed them with his army, elephants and all, to descend into Italy and defeat the Romans in battles never to be forgotten.

The army now crossing the Alps was Roman, and its commander was Emperor Constantine. But his goal, too, was Rome. For there was civil war in the year 312, the inevitable outcome of a political situation so crazy that there was nothing comparable in history.

After the death of Diocletian, emperors had seemed to shoot up like mushrooms. Just as the dying Constantius had predicted, old Maximian, not content to see Constantine and Galerius share the power of the empire, tried a comeback. He started by making his son Maxentius the ruler of Italy. But in order to do so, father and son had to get rid of Galerius' loyal man, Severus, who was already ruling there. They did away with Severus, but this move had an even more important result. The Emperor Galerius himself tried to avenge his friend and landed in Italy with a considerable army. His forces were beaten, and he retired to Nicomedia and died soon afterward.

The situation then became more complicated than ever. For a while, no fewer than six emperors divided the huge empire among them, Constantine ruling in Britain and Gaul; and few of the empire's inhabitants knew the names of all six.

Not content with giving the rule of Italy to his son,

old Maximian tried to establish himself as sole emperor again. Maxentius promptly drove him into exile. The old man fled to Gaul, where he met with Constantine and asked for asylum. Asylum was granted to him, primarily as a result of the plea of his youngest daughter, Princess Fausta, one of the more beautiful young women in the day.

Just as his father had been taken in by Maximian's eldest daughter, so now Constantine was by Fausta. And like his father, he repudiated his first wife to marry the young princess and thereby gained what power and prestige Maximian had left.

Helena was in Gaul at the time, in Arles, where the marriage was to take place. Two days before the ceremony, she left Arles and returned to Britain. She would have no part in this act of injustice. She tried hard to comfort Minervina. But Minervina was not Helena. She had been ailing before. Now her health broke down completely, and shortly afterward she died. Her son, young Crispus, remained in Helena's care till he was old enough to enter the army. It was almost a complete repetition of what had happened before. Almost.

Soon, Constantine was to find out that old Maximian still had ambitions of his own, that he had brought about the marriage to fulfill his own plans, not those of his son-in-law.

When Constantine was on a punitive expedition against the Franks, the old man spread the rumor that his son-in-law had fallen in battle. Promptly, Maximian assumed the purple for which he had been longing so many years. Once more he was an emperor.

Maximian had silenced, by bribe, a number of important officers. But not all of them. Constantine received a hurried message about what had happened and returned to capture his father-in-law before the situation got entirely out of hand. Soon afterward, despite the pleadings of the beauteous Fausta, Maximian was executed.

This gave Emperor Maxentius the pretext he needed to claim Gaul and even Britain for himself. Only a short while before, he had exiled his own father; now he pretended to be the devoted son who could not leave his father's death unavenged.

Constantine soon heard that Maxentius was doing more than uttering threats and drinking toasts "to the death and destruction of the murderer of Emperor Maximian". Maxentius was drafting soldiers all over Italy; he was planning war.

And for this purpose the long, scaly serpent was marching across the Alps. Constantine, not waiting to be attacked on his own territory, had collected as many troops as he could and was marching to forestall the attacker.

When dusk began to fall, the snake came to a standstill.

There was no need for soldiers of Constantine's cavalry units to dismount; they had been marching alongside their horses for hours on end. Nor did the infantry make camp in the systematic way they were accustomed to.

Each had to camp as best he could, and only the commanders had the luxury of a tent. Campfires were forbid-
den. From such a height, they could have been seen at a
great distance, and some of Emperor Maxentius' patrols,
though still very far away, might draw useful conclusions
at the sight of a couple of thousand campfires.

The troops grumbled, of course. After a long and
arduous march, they were longing for some warm food.
Besides, it was cold, and there was something eerie about
the stony darkness of the scenery, with the thin mists of
the evening welling up. But the grumbling was subdued
and, on the whole, no more than routine. They liked
their young leader, especially those who had been with
him in the expedition against the Franks. He had been
with them in the thick of battle during that campaign,
instead of keeping the safe position behind the lines
prescribed to Roman generals.

Their meal of dried meat and bread was interrupted
by the sound of tramping hooves and creaking wheels. A
wagon with mules was coming up the steep mountainside—in itself, nothing extraordinary. There were hundreds of such wagons with the army, carrying food and
equipment and parts of siege engines.

But this wagon was different. It was drawn by eight
mules, and yet it was a light carriage. All the mules
were carrying bundles of luggage on their backs. Behind the carriage rode an officer in armor—a centurion—and the soldiers grinned when they saw that he
was an old man, too old to be with the regular army.

The grinning ceased when they saw his many badges and decorations.

But who was in the carriage? It certainly was not the emperor. They all knew he was in front, with the vanguard.

Those nearest to it saw that the person in the carriage was a woman, a veiled woman. Those to whom they passed on the news could not believe it. What should a woman do here?

They all knew that no women were allowed to follow the army this time. Someone's suggestion that it might be the emperor's wife was greeted with hoots of laughter. It was well known that the young Empress Fausta was much too preoccupied with her clothes and cosmetics to think of following her husband on a campaign, let alone a campaign starting with so rough a passage as a crossing of the Alps. Yet she was bound to be a person of great standing, or the commanders in the rear would not have let her pass.

The carriage went on, to stop only when it reached the vanguard, where the emperor's bodyguard had pitched a few tents.

When Valentinus, his chief aide, reported that the Empress-Mother Helena had arrived, Constantine's first thought was that the man was joking. It was four years since he had last seen his mother, just before his marriage to Fausta.

Valentinus could only repeat, "Domina Flavia Julia Helena Augusta to visit the emperor."

Constantine stepped out of his tent. There she was, all gray now, and stooping just a little, but smiling. He rushed up to her, and they embraced. "What a surprise", he said. "I thought you a thousand miles away, in Britain, in Verulam, in the old house where you insisted on living. —But we can't talk here", he added hastily. He led her into his tent. He was sincerely glad to see her; yet at the same time, uneasy. It was not only that he knew of her disapproval of some of his actions, nor was it the strength of her personality. There was something about her he could not fathom, and it puzzled him.

He led her to the best seat, a field-chair with leather-covered cushions. "How tired you must be!" he said. "What can I get for you? Wine? You must be hungry too."

She shook her head. "I shall have something to eat later on. Favonius is with me. He's having my tent pitched for me. He's looking after everything for me."

"What about your ladies-in-waiting? Don't they . . . ?"

"I left them at home, of course. I can't drag *them* up the mountains and make them go on a campaign. Don't be silly."

Constantine threw back his head, laughing. "Dear Mother . . . no one has told me not to be silly, not in years and years. It's four years since I've seen you, isn't it?" In a changed tone he added, "You said you couldn't make your ladies go on a campaign. Surely you don't mean that *you* are going to come with us . . . all the way?"

"That is exactly what I mean, Son."

"But, Mother, this is war. Surely . . ."

"Of course it's war. Never mind, Son. I won't be a nuisance to you. I'm still quite strong, you know, and so is old Favonius. You don't have to worry about me in the least."

He looked at her, searchingly. "Mother, why did you come?"

She looked back firmly. "You know, of course, that you have done certain things I did not approve of—to put it mildly."

He bit his lip. "I suppose so", he said. "Minervina—."

"That's one of the things—the main thing, I should say."

"And old Maximian's death . . ."

Helena sighed. "That was the direct consequence of the first thing. One evil inevitably generates another. You hoped to gain power through your marriage to Maximian's daughter. Instead, your father-in-law almost cost you the throne."

"Almost", Constantine said grimly. "Not quite."

"May God grant that the evil consequences are at an end now", Helena said, and she gave a little shiver. "I have never written to you about these things. I could not. They had to be said. And I did not want to come to you until now. I had to wait until you were alone."

Constantine bowed his head. Strange how strong the dislike was between his mother and Fausta. His mother no doubt saw in her the woman who had ousted

Minervina. Nor was it only that Fausta was offended because Helena would not take part in the wedding ceremony. They were naturally opposed, fire and water.

"Now I have come," Helena continued, "but not only to tell you of my disapprovals. I have spoken to many of your subjects both in Britain and in Gaul, and I am charged to tell you that they love you and respect you for being a wise and good ruler."

The strong young face flushed a little. "Thank you, Mother."

"I disapprove of the other things but give you credit for the good you are doing", she said quietly.

"And . . . this war, Mother?"

"War is a terrible thing", Helena said. "But Maxentius is an evil and treacherous man. Even so, I didn't know what to think until I heard that he was persecuting the Christian community and was personally guilty of the death of the noble Sophronia, the wife of the prefect of Rome. Then I knew that God wants you to save His people."

"The God of the Christians, you mean, I take it?"

"The only God there is, Constantine."

He raised his brows. "You have become a Christian then, Mother?"

"Yes. And I pray to God for forgiveness that it has taken me such a long time. I was a fool, a proud fool."

Constantine shook his head. "Father left as his last order that I should make good what injustice had been done to the Christians. So I had to occupy my mind with that question. I know something about what Christians believe—of what you believe, Mother. I hope you will forgive me for being utterly frank. I can't believe as you do—I mean, about God becoming man and being born from a virgin and living among men and dying on the cross to redeem the world. It is all very beautiful and touching, Mother, but it's so unlikely, isn't it? That and the story about paradise and the serpent . . . it's a Jewish story. It isn't Roman. It has nothing to do with us."

He stood up and walked over to his field-desk. "I know Rome is far from perfect", he said. "We have produced terrible men in the course of our history, but also the finest. And that goes not only for statesmen and soldiers, but also for culture and art. Livius to me is as great a historian as the Greeks Herodotus or Thucydides. And Virgil as great a poet as Homer. I was reading the *Aeneid* only last night. Virgil sings of arms and a hero, Mother. That is my world, not the story of the poor little Jew."

He thumped the scrolls on his desk. "I hope you won't be angry with me, Mother. You know I'll do everything I can for your Christians, even if I shall never be one of them."

She said calmly, "As the emperor you can do much—but it is as nothing compared with what Christ can do for you." She rose. "I am tired."

"I shall come with you, Mother; to see Favonius again, too."

The old soldier received them with a smart salute,

standing in front of Helena's newly pitched tent. "All ready for you, Domina Augusta." He had never failed to call her that since the dying Constantius had conferred that supreme title on her.

She gave him a gracious nod, smiled at her son, and walked into the tent. Constantine stayed on for a few moments to speak with his one-time teacher.

"Thank you for all you have done for my mother."

"To serve her is joy, my Emperor. But—may I ask a favor?"

"It is granted before you tell me what it is."

"I wish to fight at your side when it comes time to do battle."

"Favonius! You aren't as young as you used to be, you know—and this time—"

"Only seventy-two, my Emperor. Strong as a horse. If it would please you to have another little fencing bout with me?"

Constantine laughed aloud. "I don't think I've forgotten any of the tricks you taught me. Well, I've been imprudent enough to grant your wish before it was uttered, so: What can I do? But you are my mother's servant, not mine. I'll let you fight at my side if she'll permit it."

Favonius grinned hugely. "It's all right then, sir. I asked her first, and she told me she'll permit it if you will."

Laughing again, Constantine returned to his tent. The oil lamp shone on the scrolls on his desk. The *Aeneid*,

Virgil's epic: He would do a little reading. Good for washing away those tales of a "Jewish god".

He took up the nearest scroll and read:

"Ye Sicilian Muses—let us sing of higher things . . ." That wasn't the *Aeneid*, though. It was Virgil, but it wasn't the *Aeneid*.

> *The great series of ages begins anew. . . .*
> *Now, too, returns the virgin Astraea,*
> *Returns the reign of Saturn.*
> *Now a young progeny is sent down*
> *From high heaven.*

What? A new age to begin, and a new child to be sent to earth from high heaven, born of a virgin?

Constantine shook his head. He had to forget about that Jewish tale. This was Virgil, Roman of the Romans.

> *Be thou but propitious to the infant boy*
> *Under whom first the iron age shall cease*
> *And the golden age all over the world arise. . . .*

Virgil's Fourth Eclogue—dedicated to the Consul Pollio, under the rule of Augustus, three hundred years ago or a little more.

> *Under thy conduct*
> *Whatever vestiges of our guilt remain*
> *Shall be done away,*
> *The earth released from fear forever;*
> *He shall partake of the life of the gods,*
> *Shall see heroes join the society of gods,*

Himself be seen by them,
And rule the peaceful world
With his father's virtues. . . .

The son of Jove, of the supreme God, to be born from a virgin and appear on earth to cleanse it from guilt! But *that* was what these Christians believed! Pale and with trembling fingers, Constantine read on. The poet praised the new world where all poisons would vanish:

The serpent also shall die.

He read on, as in a fever. The golden age would not be peace at once. There would be trouble—some marks of the ancient vice would remain, and wars would be fought. But in the end, the ultimate end, the world would be saved. All this, Virgil wrote—when?

Constantine thought it over. Virgil died in the year 734 of the foundation of Rome. And the Christians claimed that their Christ was born about fifteen or twenty years later.

The emperor remembered the maxim: *A true poet is also a true prophet.* Could it be that Virgil had foreseen the coming of that strange being whom Christians called the Anointed One, the Christ?

Not an hour before, Constantine had told his mother that Virgil and Rome were his world—not stories about her Christ. And now he saw Virgil himself pointing to Christ.

10

BY THIS SIGN . . .

I N THE BASILICA OF VERONA, Helena was praying
before a large cross of dark wood. It was about the
size the Cross of Jesus must have been.

The bishop of Verona had had it erected in memory
of the Christian martyrs. At long last, the Christian community could use their church again. Up till a week
before, it had been a storehouse for Maxentius' troops.

So far, all had gone well for Constantine's campaign. The crossing of the Alps now seemed to have been months ago, so much had happened since. He had stormed the mountain fortifications; he had beaten two of Maxentius' generals, at Turin and at Verona.

But now he was marching on Rome with an army weakened by losses that could not be replaced. And there, Maxentius was awaiting him with his main forces. According to intelligence reports, Maxentius had three men for every man that Constantine could put into the field.

In her heart and mind, Helena was with them. Their troubles and worries, their toil and dangers, as well as her own, she laid before the Cross. "Look down on me", she prayed, "You Who were troubled and worried, You Who toiled and were in danger. I'm only an old woman, worth nothing; but I speak to you for them, for every one of them—and first and foremost for my own son. . . . He is the head and mind of his army, as You are the Head of the Church and its Heart and Soul. Despite the fact that he does not as yet acknowledge You as his Master as I do, listen to the prayer of Your handmaid and make him the instrument of Your will, so that through him Your people will be free to worship You all over the empire. . . ."

At the war council, Constantine alone was his usual breezy self, full of confidence and strength. He had given his commanders his idea of the battle. It would be a battle of the wings—which meant that the brunt of it would have to be borne by the cavalry.

The commanders did not like it. Legate Asclepiodatus warned that the enemy had three cavalry units to one of Constantine's.

"True. But they only have two types: the light Numidians, on small horses and without any armor; and the very heavy cavalry, armored so strongly that they can't maneuver."

Vindorix, the commander of Constantine's Gallic Cavalry, said sullenly, "They can't maneuver much, but they're very difficult to dislodge."

Asclepiodatus argued that so near to Rome, their last and most powerful stronghold, Maxentius' troops would fight much better than in previous encounters—especially as they had the Praetorian Guards with them, the elite of all Roman troops.

"That's what they were once," Constantine retorted, "but now they're no more than show pieces. They *look* good, that's all. What's come over all of you? One more victory, and the war is over."

Legate Asclepiodatus scratched his gray head. "Nothing's come over us, my Emperor. But what's going to come over us tomorrow is an army of a hundred forty thousand. And we're a bare forty thousand."

"One of my seasoned men is worth more than six of Maxentius' draftees", Constantine said with a shrug.

But he knew that he could not shrug away the spiritlessness that seemed to have taken possession of his council. He dismissed them curtly, and they slunk off silently, hesitantly. He did not like his situation at all.

The next day would decide everything. At day's end, either he or Maxentius would be emperor. There was no doubt that Maxentius could stay in Rome and let himself be besieged, as the better strategy. For an army of forty thousand to succeed in a siege against a city defended by more than three times that number was next to impossible, especially as Rome had had several months to fill its silos and warehouses with supplies. Not even Hannibal, after his victory at Cannae, had been able to overcome Rome's defenses.

But instead, from all intelligence reports received by Constantine, it was clear that Maxentius was coming out of his gigantic shell, in full force, against him. This was the opportunity.

Constantine understood some of what was going on in the minds of his commanders. It was not the size of the enemy forces that frightened them, nor was it Maxentius' generalship. It was *Rome*. To them, Rome was the unconquerable, the undefeatable, the very symbol of victory. A Roman army could be defeated. Rome could not.

Constantine too saw that he was up against something of that spirit. If only he had been able to take his entire army with him from Britain and Gaul. But if he had done so, the wild Scots would have jumped over the northern wall to take control of Britain, and the Franks also would have come from the north to overrun Gaul, with no one to stop them. Maxentius, perhaps, would not have had such scruples.

Was it true, then, that Astraea, symbol of justice, had left the earth in despair, as the legend said? Or was it true what Virgil sang, that she had returned and given birth to a son who would bring back the golden age? And was it true, as Mother thought, that the prophecy meant her Christ?

He smiled grimly. If his army did not win tomorrow, the fate of the Christians in the empire would be sealed. Maxentius would see to that. So the Christian god at least (thought Constantine) should be on his side . . . if such a god existed at all. Mother, of course, was sure of that . . .

He sauntered toward the entrance of the tent. There he found Valentinus, his chief aide, staring at the sky.

The sun was setting. But high above it was another light, a strange, long beam of fire—no, two beams, crossing . . . A cross of fire.

Next to him, Valentinus also was staring up at the luminous appearance. His lips were moving. What was he doing—praying?

"Valentinus."

"My Emperor?"

"Are you a Christian, by any chance?"

"Yes, my Emperor."

"And . . . does *this* mean anything to you?"

"It's a cross, my Emperor."

Constantine said nothing. Instead he turned and went back into his tent. Orderlies brought him his supper, but he did not feel hungry. He threw himself on his field-bed and began to think through once again his battle plan. Maxentius was coming out; some of his troops had already crossed the Tiber. He was going to give battle with the Tiber to his rear. He would have to ferry over the rest of his troops during the night, or perhaps in the very early hours of the morning. Constantine thought: I shall have to attack early, before all his forces are over. Then, when the bridges are congested . . .

It had been a strange appearance—a cross of fire, a cross of light . . .

He woke and sat up. "By this sign thou shalt conquer", he said aloud. And again, in a lower voice, "By this sign thou shalt conquer."

Who had said that to him? He must have dreamed something. Who could have said it? Or had he seen it written in the sky?

The sky! The cross of light in the sky!

He jumped to his feet. "Valentinus! Valentinus!"

Valentinus came in, still half in sleep, but sword in hand. "My Emperor?"

"Take tablet and stylus. Write: General order to the army. Every officer and man will have a white cross painted on his helmet and on his shield."

Valentinus looked at him, bewildered. "Write, man", Constantine snapped. "Next: long white pennants will be carried on the pikes. On these pennants there will be a Greek *chi*." The letter *chi*, X, in the form of a cross, was the first letter of *Chrestos*, the Christ.

Valentinus wrote. He was beaming. Constantine went on: "Crosses will be painted also on the standards of the cavalry. The troops will rise two hours before dawn." After a moment he added: "No official explanation will be given about this order. Have you got it all? Off with you."

Valentinus rushed out, still beaming. There was no need to give the men an explanation. They would be shrewd enough to connect the cross on helmets and shields with the strange omen most of them were bound to have seen in the sky.

They were. When the painting parties arrived, immediately after the breakfast of *pulsum* (porridge) and the usual mixture of water and a little vinegar to drink, many legionaries thought the white crosses were a new kind of spell. Others knew for certain that the paint contained some magic concoction that would make their shields safe against arrows and spear-thrusts. And some men—those with connections—had heard that the emperor had been promised a great victory by some god if his men would fight under the new emblem.

But about one-tenth of the army was Christian, and to them the matter was clear: the emperor had become a Christian himself, and that meant that the whole empire would be. They were beside themselves with joy, and their joy was infectious. Few soldiers still devoutly believed in the old gods, though some of them grumbled when they saw the Roman eagles replaced by the new standards with the *chi*. The Christians, of course, under-stood at once, and their enthusiasm rose to a frenzy that affected even those who had never heard of Christ.

The general feeling was that the emperor seemed to have made an alliance with some new and powerful god and that those among them who knew something about that god were absolutely certain that this meant a complete and decisive victory. Perhaps they were right. In any case, the emperor, so far, had always known what he was doing. . . .

They cheered him when he appeared on his chestnut horse, with a golden cross painted on his helmet and shield, and followed by his bodyguards wearing the same emblem.

Constantine smiled, waved, and rode on to the van-tage point he had chosen: a prominence of reddish rock from which the place took its name—*Saxa Rubra*. From here he could see before him the vast plain through which the Tiber lazily made its way. On his right, the Gallic cavalry was taking up formation.

"Valentinus!"

"My Emperor?"

"I want only the first wave of the Gallic cavalry to be visible. The second and third will keep behind the rocks. Quickly.'"

Valentinus dispatched an aide. At least fifty aides were standing ready, behind the emperor and his staff, and theirs were the best horses of all. ("My lightnings", Con-stantine liked to call them.)

Favonius appeared as from nowhere, and the emperor smiled. "As good as your word, I see. Friends, this is Marcus Favonius, First Centurion of the Twentieth under my father. He taught me everything I know about swordplay. —Keep on my right side, Favonius. Anything to report?"

"The Eighth Legion is in position behind the Gallic cavalry, my Emperor", Favonius said briefly.

Constantine nodded. "That's where I ordered them to be."

Favonius pursed his lips. He said nothing but looked straight ahead. There, at a distance of three miles or so, the plain was glittering in the morning sun: armor, heavy armor, Maxentius' pride—his *cataphractarii*, man and horse armored from head to foot. Behind them . . . nothing—nothing but the Tiber. Of course, all knew that it was next to impossible to dislodge them. The *cataphractarii* were virtual fortresses on horseback. So: Maxentius was using his left wing defensively. Either he would attack Constantine's left wing, or he would try to break his center. A frontal attack would be much more costly, of course, but Maxentius could well afford it, the odds being three or even four to one—if he could get enough troops across the Tiber. But if he was clever, he would try to turn Constantine's left wing—turn it and roll up the entire position.

Favonius looked to the left. The battle was on over there. Huge columns of dust were darkening the sky. Apparently Asclepiodatus had made an attack. There were long glittering lines still on the other side of the Tiber, and only two bridges, a small one and the large Milvian Bridge.

An aide came up in a thundering gallop. "Report from Legate Vindorix: the enemy's light cavalry has suffered about one thousand dead and is beginning to waver. They'll break in less than one hour unless reinforcements come in."

"Very good", Constantine said calmly.

Another aide came racing up. "Report from Legate Trebonius, my Emperor. The Praetorian Guards are approaching the Tiber and will cross on the Milvian Bridge."

Constantine nodded. "Stay and fight with us, Faber. You, too, Aufidius."

Favonius grinned to himself. He remembered the very day when the late Emperor Constantius, then a mere legate, had taught his little son that a commander in the field must always remember the names of all of his officers.

"Valentinus!"

"My Emperor?"

"Order to Legate Asclepiodatus: the Tenth and Twenty-First will attack in the direction of the Milvian Bridge in one hour's time."

"Yes, my Emperor."

Favonius made a few hasty calculations. In one hour no more than about half of the Praetorians would be over the bridge. He grinned to himself again. Then he thought of the Gallic cavalry, and of the Eighth Legion hiding behind them, and gave a low whistle. Some of the staff officers looked shocked, but the emperor smiled.

"Guessed something, old war dog, have you?"

"Maybe I have, my Emperor", Favonius said, beaming. "But it's a new trick. I never taught you that one."

Constantine gave a short laugh. Again he looked toward the left. The dust columns were moving toward the Tiber. Legate Vindorix was driving the enemy's Numidian cavalry before him.

"Valentinus! Give the signal for the first wave of the Gallic cavalry. No more than the first wave, understand?"

"Yes, my Emperor." Valentinus sent off an orderly. Three thousand men on horseback waved their lances and began to move.

The staff officers looked anxiously at Constantine. It seemed madness to send only three thousand men against the *cataphractarii*. They would be slaughtered, down to the last man, for they were one against five, to say nothing of the difference in armor.

The Gallic cavalry had fallen into a trot. Soon they would gallop.

Even Favonius was holding his breath. Three thousand good men less, he thought.

"Valentinus! The second and third wave."

"Yes, my Emperor. —Rush off, Aulus, as quickly as you can."

"Valentinus! The Eighth Legion is to follow up the attack."

That was it, Favonius thought. A surprise attack, cavalry and regular infantry against the static wing of the enemy . . .

The first wave of the Gallic cavalry was galloping straight into the tremendous mass of iron waiting for them. There was no penetration. On the contrary, whole rows of the attackers seemed to have been thrown off their horses.

But Constantine knew the real reason for that. He had personally trained the officers of the Gallic cavalry for the fight against armored cavalry. The men jumped off their mounts, crawled under the bellies of the enemy horses, and butchered them off from underneath with their long daggers.

He could see something like a slight weaving going on within the first rows of the enemy.

And now the second wave of the Gallic cavalry was thundering by. Their task was different; they had to crash through what gaps the first wave had made for them.

Constantine sat up in the saddle. "Valentinus! All the guards, follow me. Trumpeters, give the signal for attack. We're moving in between the second and third waves." He rode off. At once Favonius drew his sword and followed.

Valentinus shouted the orders. The bodyguards spurred their horses and broke ranks as they went down from the red rocks to reach their emperor and form a living wall around him. The dust whirled up by the second wave of the Gallic cavalry formed a dark curtain before them. There was a low, thunderous noise behind them, where the third wave was breaking into a trot and then into a gallop.

A terrible, splintering crash before them: the second wave had broken into the enemy formation. If they could split it right through, they would veer and break up the slow-moving *cataphractarii* from the rear.

The bodyguards galloped into a narrow channel, almost a hundred yards deep, to be greeted by a hail of spears. Grunting, Favonius hacked some of them off his shield. The world was full of helmets and spears and arms lifted to strike, of shrieks and bellows and the long-drawn death cries of horses. Here, there, everywhere, Maxentius' one-man fortresses were down, and the men of the first wave were killing them off, one by one.

Some of the bodyguards went down under a hail of missiles. Valentinus, shielding the emperor, was hit in the shoulder.

Constantine was too busy fighting to see it. He was trying a different technique from that prescribed to the first wave. Not for him the jump from the horse, the crawling under an enemy horse, and the dagger-thrust up. He drew up as close to his adversary as he could and thrust his short, broad blade into his throat, just where the helmet ended and the shoulder armor had not yet begun. The thing demanded much precision, and he killed three of the *cataphractarii* that way while Favonius was warding off death a dozen times and more at his sword side.

The sight of the emperor himself hacking his way through made his men fighting mad. They pressed on and on, despite the heavy losses they suffered. Even so, the second wave of the Gallic cavalry did not quite succeed in its task to split the terrible enemy formation in two. There was a bulge within its last third, pulsating and erupting in all directions.

But with a crash the third wave plunged into the fray, and behind them the first lines of the Eighth became visible, a tightly compressed wall of steel advancing.

The commanders of the armored cavalry saw them. They knew there was no chance of finishing off the Gallic cavalry before the Eighth arrived. They turned their heavy horses and fled. Their men followed as best they could, first a trickle, then a stream, those who managed to escape the relentless attackers.

At once Constantine stopped fighting. "Trumpeters!" It was not easy to find them, for they had joined in the battle, but his staff brought up two of them.

"Signal B", Constantine ordered them. "Re-form!" They had to repeat it three times until the men stopped pursuing the fugitives and obeyed.

"Re-form! Re-form!"

When they had done so, Constantine sent half of them after the retreating enemy. "Don't fight them.

Drive them before you; drive them into the Tiber. But stay in formation."

"They'll crash into their own infantry", Favonius said. "And if they try to use the bridge, it will collapse . . ."

"I hope so", Constantine said cheerfully.

"Now I know why you ordered Legate Asclepiodatus to attack in that direction", Favonius said, and there was awe in his tone and expression. "How I wish I were fifty years younger—there are things I could learn from *you*!"

The emperor laughed and looked on a while as the other half of his men rounded up prisoners. When the Eighth Legion arrived, he rode up to them. "They've left no work for you here", he said. "But I shall see to it that you get work soon enough." He told the legate in command to detail five hundred men to take charge of the prisoners and to follow him with the others. The legate grinned all over his leathery face. "I think I know what you want us to do, my Emperor. You want us to give them a swimming lesson."

"Exactly."

When the prisoners—almost two thousand of them— were secured, Constantine sent the rest of the Gallic cavalry to follow after the first wave, and he followed at the head of the Eighth Legion.

At the Milvian Bridge, the congestion was so terrible that many of Maxentius' men died from suffocation. The fleeing *cataphractarii*, who, in their heavy armor, could not dare to swim the river, had all made for the bridge; they had overrun several infantry contingents to reach it. But on the bridge itself, they ran into the mounted Praetorians, and that proved too much for it. As Favonius had thought and Constantine hoped, the bridge collapsed, and hundreds of Maxentius' best men fell into the water. A few managed to keep afloat for a while; fewer still, to save themselves.

But the Praetorian infantry, and with them the other elite troops that had reached the plain of Saxa Rubra, still stood their ground.

Vindorix had driven the Numidians to flight but was stopped by the six legions Maxentius had got across the Tiber. He was intelligent enough to wait until Asclepio-datus attacked. Then only, he joined in.

Even so, there was little progress on either side, partly because of the bravery of Maxentius' troops but also because they were so close together that there was no room for maneuvering.

Then the Gallic cavalry arrived, and Constantine with the Eighth.

Maxentius' men saw before them an imposing semi-circle of enemies, white crosses on helmets and shields glistening in the sun, strange banners raised against them. It was not surprising, perhaps, that on the day after the battle the rumor went around in Rome that an army of "warriors of light" had come to the help of Constantine and had decided the day for him and his cause.

The battle had started as a fight between the cavalry on both wings. Now two tightly pressed masses of men were slaughtering each other.

Half of Maxentius' men were still on the other side of the Tiber, with no hope of joining their hard-pressed comrades. The second, smaller bridge had broken down, too. And worst of all, news reached them that Maxentius himself had been on the Milvian Bridge when it fell and that he had drowned in the Tiber.

Somehow the news seeped through to the other side, and, like a wind-blown spark, jumped over to Constantine's troops.

"Maxentius is dead", Constantine roared, and the word spread quickly. But the troops of Maxentius would not lay down their arms even then. Furious, Constantine himself led another attack against them, then a second, then a third. Twice his horse was brought down from under him by volleys of arrows. In the third attack, old Favonius went down. Constantine came to his side. At a glance he saw that his old teacher and friend was dying.

Favonius said, "Tell . . . Domina Helena . . . I guarded . . . you . . . well." Then the life went out of his eyes, and Constantine wept openly. He ordered the old man's body carried to the back lines. "Tomorrow we shall bury him in Rome."

He mounted again, only to perceive that the fight was over. At long last, the legions of Maxentius surrendered—the Second, Fourth, Seventeenth, and Nineteenth Legions and the Praetorian cohorts.

That same day, Constantine and his forces entered Rome in triumph.

ONLY ONE EMPEROR

T HIRTEEN YEARS after the battle of Milvian Bridge, Helena, in her quiet home at Verulam, received a startling message from her son. It was sent from Byzantium, now renamed Constantinople and the official second capital of the empire.

Much had happened in these thirteen years, and almost all of it was good. After the defeat and death of Maxentius, Constantine had proclaimed the Edict of

Milan, restoring to the Christians of the empire the rights former emperors had taken away from them. Indeed, Christianity was now the officially recognized religion of the state.

Helena herself had entered Rome soon after the victory, and, with a small army of voluntary helpers, she set up organizations and institutions unknown so far in the entire world. Special houses were built and staffed for the sick, and it made no difference whether or not they were able to pay for their quarters, food, and treatment. Schools were founded for those who wished to be instructed in the Christian faith.

The entire system of inns in Italy and Gaul was reorganized, enabling travelers to find rest and refreshment without fear of being robbed in their sleep or having to put up with other undesirable aspects for which inns had become notorious. "Christ taught us that what we do for the least of our neighbors, we do for Him", Helena said. "Therefore, every guest, every stranger, must be received as if he were Christ."

Her special care was dedicated to the poor, and so frequent were her demands that Constantine, despite the huge treasures he found in Rome, was sometimes at a loss to know how to meet them. But still it was easier to find the means somewhere than to resist the energetic old lady.

Only when her organizations and institutions were running smoothly did she return to her beloved Britain and to the peace of her house. Wherever she had gone, a multitude of churches grew up from the foundation stones she laid.

She did not participate in the campaign Constantine launched against Licinius, emperor of the East, around whom the pagan elements had gathered with a view to reconquering the West for him and the ancient gods. She knew her son would be victorious, and he was. After Constantine's victories at Hadrianople and Chalcedon, the captive Licinius committed suicide.

And now at long last the word was fulfilled that Constantine once spoke to his dying father: "There should be only one emperor." He was the sole ruler from Britain to Persia, from Germany to Africa.

Only one thing was missing in Helena's joy and peace: Constantine, to whom Christ had given so much, had not himself become a Christian. "Not yet", he said whenever she tried to persuade him to be baptized. And he smiled in a way that was puzzling to her, as if he had some particular reason he did not wish to explain. Yet he knew how important baptism was. He knew a great deal now about the Christian religion, and it was he who had made possible a great council of the Church, the Council in Nicaea.

The year before, that council had begun, and, under the guidance of wise bishops and especially Athanasius of Alexandria, had made much progress.

But not all of the issues had been resolved or even discussed, among them being the sacrament of confession. Some Christian leaders advocated that the remission of sins could be given only once in this life, and that any relapse into the same sins was unforgivable. Surely that could not be so, others argued. If one was to forgive one's brother not seven, but seventy times seven times, could not at least equal mercy be expected from God, Who was Mercy itself?

Perhaps it was this question that kept Constantine from asking to be baptized—the fear that he might again commit a sin he had committed in the past. Was he waiting until, in his dying hour, he felt safe enough to rid himself of all guilt?

Again Helena scanned the letter she had received from Constantinople, a strange, confused letter in which Constantine wrote about "certain dangers" in his "most intimate surrounding", saying that he would have to cope with them, and that he did not know quite how to do it. He made allusions to persons near to him, who owed everything to his "magnanimity and good will", and yet who answered with "glaring ingratitude and even with the spirit of revolt and of deception, which no man could tolerate, and least of all the emperor".

At the end he wrote about how much he regretted that he could not discuss these vital issues with his "wise and saintly mother", as they demanded his continued presence in the capital; and he could not burden her, at her age, with such a long and arduous journey.

Helena frowned. She had passed her seventy-fourth year of life, but she hated being told that she could no longer go on a journey, even a long and arduous one, when her help was needed. And she felt sure that it was needed. She did not like the way in which Constantine explained things without explaining them at all. *Who* were these people he complained about, and *what* were they really up to? And who had told him about it all? There were always many people at court who would try to gain prestige and power by denouncing their betters, and they could be so glib about it. Could it be that the empress . . . ? But Constantine had spoken of more than one person.

Helena rose. With her black cane, she tapped the floor vigorously. When Terentia, her lady-in-waiting, appeared, she said, "We're leaving for Rome. Pack my things and yours. The barest necessities, Terentia, none of your vases and things. Send a dispatch rider to Anderida. I want a ship. I don't care what sort of ship it is, large or small, as long as it is large enough to get us over the channel at once. To Gessiacum. From there we shall travel overland. I want my carriage to be ready in two hours. Now, repeat to me what I said so that I can be sure there won't be the usual confusion."

It was a long and arduous journey, despite the fact that Helena could now enjoy some of the fruits of her own achievements, the well-working, clean, and decent state inns all along the way. She made use of an assumed name. It would not have been right for the empress-mother to travel without retinue and escort, and she did not wish to be slowed by the usual "Imperial Progress" involving solemn receptions at every town, speeches, banquets, and all the rest that imperial etiquette demanded.

But when at last she arrived at Constantinople, she found that she had come too late. One week before she arrived, young Crispus, Constantine's son by his marriage with Minervina, had been executed for high treason. And two days before Helena's arrival, the Empress Fausta had died. The official explanation was that she had succumbed to the steam of an over-heated bath. (But many suspected that her death was no accident.)

When Helena stood before her son, he admitted: "I killed her, Mother. I killed her. I had Crispus executed, and I killed Fausta. My son and my wife. And Maximian before them. Mother, Mother, why do I do such things?"

This was no longer the strong, self-confident warrior, the victor of the battle of Milvian Bridge, of Hadrianople and Chalcedon, the sole ruler of the empire. He was now a poor, despairing creature, with sunken eyes and deep furrows on forehead and cheeks, pale, trembling . . .

Helena decided that she had not come entirely too late, that she had come in time at least for her own son.

She sat down, and at once he knelt beside her, burying his head in her lap as he had done when he was a child. "Tell me what troubles you." she said.

"Mother, I can't, I . . ."

"Yes. Tell me."

He told her, not at once and not coherently, but an hour or so later she knew the facts—or, at least, the facts as he saw them. Young Crispus had done well in the two battles of the eastern campaign, and success had gone to his head. He gave himself airs, spoke of what he would do when one day he would be emperor.

Fausta, naturally preferring to have one of her own children ascend the throne instead of Minervina's son, hated Crispus for it. Very carefully she saw to it that everything that Crispus said and did was reported to Constantine in a very exaggerated manner.

The "evidence" collected against Crispus by the Security Police might have been true or false. Most likely it was false, and most likely Fausta had a hand in that, as well. But so strong was her influence then on the emperor that he believed her when she joined the young man's accusers. According to their report, Crispus in fact tried to hire men to murder his father.

Constantine appointed the sterner of his judges to examine the charge; they were only too willing to show their loyalty to the emperor by condemning the young fool to death. He was executed at Pola, in Istria.

But soon afterward, Constantine found out, through his own spies and informers, that Fausta was boasting of having brought about Crispus' downfall with clever tricks. He learned also that she had been deceiving him for years. He could not very well put her on trial, however, without exposing his own weakness toward her and his injustice in condemning Crispus. Besides, he was in such a rage that his vengeance just could not wait. He had her killed in her bath by having the room over-heated until the very floor was glowing and crumbling away. The doors, of course, were locked, and the bath attendants were replaced by soldiers sworn to secrecy.

"You are the emperor", Helena said. "That means that no one can make you responsible for these deeds; you are beyond all human jurisdiction. But you, you cannot acquit yourself, and you are responsible to God. Your deeds cannot be undone. So you must atone for them by action in the service of God, ceaseless action, as long as you still live. Don't lie here moaning and wailing. *Work*, work for the well-being of the peoples over whom you rule."

She sighed deeply. "There was a time when I hoped that the peace of Christ would rule the empire . . . through you. But how can that be so, if you yourself violate His laws?"

Then, and for no apparent reason, she thought intently of Albanus. She could see his gentle face, she could hear him say, as he did that last time he came to see her at her house in Verulam, "The Cross is the Tree of Life. . . . The Cross of our Lord has vanished. No one knows where it is. Yet the saying goes that the teaching of our Lord will encompass the Roman world only when it has been found again."

And she felt again, as she had felt then, the strong, tumultuous beating of her heart, like a wild gong thundering and thundering until her very heartbeat seemed to fill the world. The vivid memory had dissolved before she was fully aware of it.

"Mother!" Constantine was saying to her. "Mother, are you ill?"

She shook her head. After a moment she said, "At long last I understand. When you made the Cross of our Lord the emblem of your troops, I thought the old saying was fulfilled and that the rule of Christ over the empire had begun. But that was not enough. Christ will never be satisfied with mere symbols. With Him it is reality that matters. I must find the Cross, His Cross, the Cross of Golgotha."

"But, Mother, it's been lost for centuries. How can you possibly hope to find it?"

"I shall find it if that is His will", she said firmly. "And I think it is. But, for this I must have your help. I must have power, power without any limits. I want ships, men, money. Will you give them to me, . . . Emperor?"

Constantine bowed his head deeply. "You will have the ships, the men, and the money", he said, profoundly moved. "But the power must come from a higher Source than from me."

THE TRUE CROSS

T HERE WAS NO DOUBT that Bishop Macarius was
the most plagued man in Jerusalem. Ever since
the emperor had made Christianity the religion of
the state, he had been overworked. Suddenly, multi-
tudes of people were seeking to become Christians. And
it was not always easy to find out whether this wish
came from an inner conviction or a desire for promotion
and worldly advantage. It might be a good idea, some

thought, to adopt the religion apparently so dear to the ruling emperor.

All persecution of Christians had ceased, yes, but new dangers appeared and threatened. Formerly, a Christian had had to conceal his faith to avoid being jeered, abused, denounced, and put in jail. Now suddenly his religion was being proclaimed as the one true faith. Such a drastic change could too easily go to his head, and in many cases it did. The result was often arrogance, pride, and even vindictiveness—not attitudes to be desired in a Christian!

And there were Church councils, conferences, theological debates about many points of importance, which had to be clarified and decided upon; there was widespread correspondence with fellow bishops, at last no longer endangered by spies. Bishop Macarius had work enough for three bishops, and he did not know how he was to cope with it.

And then there was the empress-mother. She had arrived in Jerusalem the summer before, from Caesarea, where she had landed with half a dozen ships, full of advisers, theologians, architects, experts on Judaea, investigators, and agents. She had made her headquarters in Jerusalem and let loose her army of experts and assistants on the city to question everybody about Golgotha and the Cross of Christ.

She herself had enlisted the help of Bishop Macarius. But all he could tell her was that, according to Roman law, a man executed was to be buried at the site of execution, along with the implements by which he was killed. But, because of the intervention by Joseph of Arimathea, the Body of Jesus was not buried on Golgotha, but in a tomb belonging to the rich man. The Cross and the nails would certainly have been buried on Mount Calvary, on Golgotha.

The question, therefore, was only: Where was Mount Calvary? No one knew.

"Then I shall have to find out where it was", the elderly lady declared. "I have come here to find the Cross and to build a church on Mount Calvary, and I shall not leave Jerusalem before I have done so."

In vain, Bishop Macarius tried to point out to her that Jerusalem was ringed by hills and hillocks, any one of which might have been Mount Calvary; that other hills and hillocks had been flattened by many earthquakes in the preceding centuries; that the city had been utterly destroyed when Emperor Titus conquered it; and that the new city had a different form altogether.

His arguments made no impression on her. The investigators and agents continued to roam the city, inquiring and discussing in all the inns, in the shops, and on the squares. They spoke to Christian priests and to Jewish rabbis; to merchants, soldiers, camel drivers, and thieves; to physicians, sailors, innkeepers, teachers, philosophers, and pickpockets. Whatever could be regarded as a clue was followed up avidly by the empress-mother—avidly, and often drastically. Had there been a hillock here, in the Street of the Coppersmiths? Then the houses where it stood had to be cleared, the people living there were to be given new and better houses at imperial expense, and the place had to be dug up.

After a few months, hundreds of workmen were employed digging up places in and around Jerusalem. After six months, there were more than two thousand diggers. Everybody who had no other work was hired to dig. At the same time, new hostelries and an orphanage were built on the empress-mother's orders.

The municipal authorities did not know whether to bless the astonishing old lady or to curse her. She was upsetting the entire city, but she was also giving bread to thousands and doing more for the welfare of the poor than all the Roman authorities of the last three centuries had done together.

Behind her back, Helena was called a fool, a saint, an interfering old woman, a benefactress, and a high-handed matriarch. She knew about such talk, of course, for that also was reported to her. She did not care a straw. And despite her age, she herself made excursions, both in the city and without, accompanied, as often as not, by only a couple of ladies-in-waiting or even only with her faithful Terentia, also now elderly.

The chief of police had her followed by a number of his men. After all, he was responsible for her safety. She had him called to her and told him bluntly: "I won't have this nonsense. I want to talk to simple people, and when they see policemen sneaking along behind me they'll be afraid to talk."

Then she gave him a codicil exonerating him from any responsibility if anything should happen to her. "Now go home", she told him, "and send your police after thieves or suchlike, not after me."

Spring came to Jerusalem, and Helena was as busy as ever. Digging was going on in a dozen new places—without success, as usual. All of the work, so far, had been in vain. Helena was as little discouraged as if she had arrived the day before, instead of ten months before.

"She'll go on for years", the chief of police told Bishop Macarius. "She's seventy-five, nearly seventy-six, but she'll live to be ninety or a hundred. She won't stop, and she won't die, until she has dug up the whole of the city. You and I will be in our graves long before that. She is mad, raving mad."

"Oh, I don't think so", the bishop replied mildly.

"What do you mean? You know as well as I do that it's perfectly hopeless to find that . . . that Cross."

"You never know", said Macarius. Then he laughed. "I admit, she is as . . . overwhelming to me as she is to you. Every day I am called to the palace—to her head-quarters, I mean—to be told about new places, new ideas, new people who have made this or that suggestion. I have never seen such energy in anybody, not in all my life. But she is doing no harm to anyone and a great deal of good to many. And there is just that chance—however small, perhaps very small—that she may succeed."

"She's gotten around you", the chief of police

groaned. "She is getting around everybody. Yesterday she was in the worst district of the city—a place where even my men never go alone—with only that woman Terentia. And today she is off again, somewhere outside of the city. If anything should happen to her, how much do you think that piece of paper she gave me will help when the emperor pounces on me for letting his mother be killed by some cutthroat who smelled the gold in her purse? I have aged ten years these last ten months."

Helena was stomping across the sweet-smelling grass, with Terentia at her heels. They had brought with them young Simon, who had been their guide before, a boy of fifteen with a crippled arm. Terentia felt sorry for him but was intelligent enough not to show it. For some reason, Helena seemed to have taken a fancy to the boy, and whenever she did have such a fancy she made people talk. Simon was a silent little fellow, but she got his life story out of him. He had not been born crippled. He had been hit by lightning when, in a foolish moment, he had tried to take shelter in a thunderstorm under a large tree. He might have been killed. Instead, he was knocked senseless, and, when consciousness returned, his arm, the right arm, was lifeless, withered.

He told her all, in his slow, halting Latin mixed with his native Aramaic. Helena liked listening to Aramaic. It was the language Christ had spoken on earth—Aramaic when talking to the people, Hebrew in the synagogue when He read the sacred texts and preached.

Perhaps He had looked a little like Simon when He was his age, a handsome lad with large, dark eyes and long, curly brown hair.

"Want to see more hills, lady?" the boy asked in a matter-of-fact way.

The answer was always the same. The strange old lady always wanted to see hills. Well, there were plenty here. But when they got to the next one, she might shake her head and murmur, "No, no, not here, it can't have been here." And so they went on to the next.

The lady wanted to see more hills. Simon had another two for her, not too far from here if she did not mind walking a little.

Helena did not mind. "It's a beautiful day", she said, breathing in the scent of the oleander bushes nearby. Sheep were grazing at a distance, and an elderly shepherd was watching them leisurely.

She stepped out slowly, using the black cane she now needed for walking.

"This is one of them", Simon told her, pointing at it. "That one with the cyprus tree. And over there is the other, the one with the ruins on it. My father told me it was a temple once for one of the Roman goddesses, for Venus." He smiled a little contemptuously. "One of the emperors built it," he added, "and Father says his name was Hadrian. It was a very long time ago."

Then he saw that the old lady was not listening. She stood there gazing intently toward the hill with the ruins. Her eyes were wide open, her lips trembling.

Perhaps (her companions thought) she *was* mad after all—or ill. The boy wanted to ask her whether she felt ill—and then did not dare.

Suddenly she continued on, toward the hill and up it, steep as it was. Terentia followed along, nervous to see her mistress attempt to make such a climb.

Yet how quick the lady was; the others could scarcely keep up with her.

When Simon and Terentia reached the summit, they observed that Helena's face was as white as chalk, as they stood amid the ruins and the weeds and the rubble. After a while she said, "Terentia, go back to the city. I want two hundred workmen here immediately."

The next day, Simon came back to Hadrian's ruins, to see what was going on. He now knew that the woman whose guide he had been was the empress-mother, of whom everyone was talking everywhere. It was a difficult thing to believe. Empresses and empress-mothers surely were dressed in purple, were bedecked with jewels, and wore crowns or diadems, and were carried in litters. They did not stalk through the roads on their own feet. When the empress-mother had sent her servant away to fetch two hundred workmen, Simon really had thought she was quite mad. But within two hours, the two hundred men appeared, and with them a hundred soldiers and several officials.

Later that day, when he returned home, he was told by his family that the empress-mother had given orders

to demolish the Venus temple, but no one would believe him when he said that he had been her guide!

Why was she doing these strange things?

Today, he saw that the workers had changed the place
almost beyond recognition. The soldiers had roped off
the hill, and all of the ruins were gone. Carts drawn by
oxen and mules stood loaded with rubble and broken
chunks of columns.

Simon tried to slip through the ropes, but one of the
guards shoved him back.

A very imperious old voice said, "Let that boy come
through", and the guard, looking quite sheepish, lifted
up the rope a little for him to slip through. There was
the lady nodding at him, and beside her was an oldish
man with a gentle face and a mop of gray hair, dressed as
simply as she was. The lady said to him, "This is Simon,
holy Bishop. He helped me find the place." The bishop
smiled, but he looked uneasy, as if he too did not quite
know what all this was about.

"You may come with us", the old lady said to the
boy, and he did. The three went up the hill, and there,
on the summit, the workmen were still digging. The
ruins were all gone, but they were still digging. There
was a large hole in the ground. Perhaps they were looking for a treasure?

Bishop Macarius *was* uneasy. He had been ordered
away from his work, first to the palace, then to this
place where everything was in a whirl of movement,
ropes, workers, soldiers, and gaping onlookers. The

chief of police was here, as well, looking more than ever like a disgruntled old dog, and shrugging his shoulders at the bishop when the empress-mother was not looking.

Apparently she thought she had found what she was looking for. But why should she think so? What evidence was there that this site was anything special?

The chief of police came up to the side of the bishop. "Quite crazy . . . I've been ordered out here—you too, I suppose—quite crazy."

"I don't know . . . ", Macarius said, taking thought. "There's just one thing. That temple, you know . . . Emperor Hadrian built it. And he hated Christianity. It's just possible that he had that temple built because he did not want Mount Calvary to become a center of pilgrimage for the Christians. Venus is the 'most pagan' of all goddesses. Hadrian, God forgive him, was the kind of man who might have done such a thing."

"That", the chief of police said, "is the only thing I've heard that makes any sense of it. But surely . . ." He broke off. Somebody was shouting something. The voice seemed to come from deep in the earth. There was a sudden rush of workmen toward the edge of the hole in the ground. They were milling around; no one could see anything.

But there was the voice again, a long-drawn cry: "*Wood!*"

Helena fell on her knees. Behind her, Terentia and other attending ladies followed her example.

Bishop Macarius hesitated. He stared down into the excavation. *Could it be?* It was so unlikely, so desperately unlikely. All around him there was complete silence. Even the birds and insects seemed to have become mute. The wind had ceased.

Then the old man gave a short, hoarse cry. He too fell on his knees, and with him the entire assembly—workmen, onlookers, soldiers.

From the depth of the hole, three wooden crosses came in sight, as very slowly, shaking and swerving, workmen carried them up to the surface. Two men were carrying each cross, and behind them came another four with spades and shovels. Once they were on the surface of the hill, they stood still. One was holding something that looked like a small roll of old parchment.

Helena tried to rise and could not. The bishop on one side, little Simon on the other, helped her to her feet and she stumbled forward until she stood at the foot of the three crosses.

Macarius saw the piece of parchment in the workman's hands. He recognized writing on it, of Greek, Latin, and Hebrew alphabets: IESUS NAZARENUS REX IUDAEORUM—the proclamation of Pilate, in Latin.

One of the three crosses was the *true* Cross. But which?

There seemed to be no doubt about *that* to Helena. She threw her arms around the heavy stem of one of them and kissed it fervently. Then, with a sudden movement, she grasped little Simon's shoulder, drew him toward her, and, seizing his withered arm, had him touch the stem of the Cross with it.

Simon shrieked with pain. Fire seemed to go up inside his arm. It was the lightning all over again. He struggled . . . and tore his arm away. *And the arm obeyed his will.* He stared at it, bewildered, and for the first time in seven years he saw the fingers of his right hand move. He closed them . . . opened them again. He moved his arm up, down, sideways . . .

To the people looking on, he seemed to be making the Sign of the Cross with his hand. Many were present who knew Simon, the cripple-boy. "A miracle", they whispered. "A miracle. It is truly the Cross of Christ!"

Half an hour later, they all returned to Jerusalem in solemn procession. Macarius himself, with the help of two young priests, was carrying the Cross. Helena followed, supported by young Simon, who was walking as in a dream. Most of the crowd were Christians; they were singing.

And thus the Cross that Christ had carried out of Jerusalem came back to the city.

For three days, Helena rested. Then she received Bishop Macarius. The old man bowed to her deeply. "Your faith has been greater than mine", he said humbly. "Your name will be blessed as long as the world will exist."

She frowned and made an impatient little gesture. "I want a church to be built on that hill", she said.

"I was just going to suggest it", Macarius said, smiling. "I shall get the best architects to design it . . ."

"No need for that", Helena interrupted. "The plans are all drawn up. Terentia, give them to me. They're in that capsula on the table."

The bishop shook his head. "How is that possible?" he said. "It takes weeks and even months to draw up such plans."

"I had them made in Rome before I set out to come here", Helena explained calmly.

Macarius raised his hands. "Now I understand why you succeeded in your impossible task", he said. "Yours is the faith that can move mountains."

Helena left the Holy Land a few weeks later. She took the Cross with her—except for a large piece of the stem, which she gave to Bishop Macarius.

The voyage was a hard one. Storms were raging, and once she came near to being shipwrecked.

When at last she reached the shore of Italy, she fell ill.

Emperor Constantine was then in Rome, but at the news of her arrival he traveled to the small port on the Adriatic Sea where she had landed. He kissed his mother's hand and bowed his knee before the Cross.

She smiled at him. She was too weak to say anything. Looking at her, Constantine knew that her end was approaching. Her face had shrunk almost to the size of a child's.

Terentia had to report to him about everything that

had happened in Jerusalem and especially about the glorious day of the finding of the Cross.

He listened reverently. Then he returned to his mother's room. She was sitting in her armchair. Her eyes were wide open. There was an expression of rapt tenderness on her shrunken face. But she was dead.

The day after, the emperor took her body with him to Rome, the city which her prayer had helped to reconquer for Christ.

Author's Note

The historians do not agree about the nationality and the social rank of Saint Helena. Some say that she was a British princess, the daughter of one of the many small rulers on the island, and mention as her father none other than King Cole (or Coel), the ruler of the Trinovants, a tribe on the east coast of Britain—the same King Cole whose name is memorialized in the well-known nursery rhyme: "Old King Cole was a merry old soul." But according to others, Helena was born in Drepanum, in eastern Europe, the daughter of an innkeeper.

When the learned men disagree, the writer is entitled to make his own choice. And it seemed to me that the character and bearing of that great and energetic lady were not only saintly but also princely in the finest sense. Of course, the daughter of an innkeeper might have a magnificent character, and the daughter of a king a low one. But if the real Helena was a princess by birth, I did not wish to offend her by making her in my book the daughter of an innkeeper; and if she was the daughter of an innkeeper, she will not be offended because I have described her as the daughter of a king!

All the great events of her life that I describe are historical. She was married to Constantius Chlorus, who left her to marry the emperor's daughter and later became emperor himself. She became a Christian at the time of the persecution of the Christians under Diocletian. She raised her and Constantius' son, Constantine, who later joined the army in the East and really made that tremendous ride across Europe to return to Britain and assume his father's throne. The march over the Alps, the battle of the Milvian Bridge, the conquest of Rome, the deaths of Crispus and Fausta, and Helena's finding of the True Cross—all of that is historical.

The day of the Finding of the Cross, May 2, was initially held as a feast day of the Church; later, the feast was renamed "The Exaltation of the Holy Cross", and celebrated on September 14, in memory of the consecration of the Church of the Holy Sepulcher in Jerusalem (on September 14, A.D. 335). Helena did not live to see the completion of the church built through her efforts on the site where the Cross was found.

There is no doubt that she was one of the great women of all time.

If she were with us on earth today, I think she would say: "I have found the True Cross of our Lord. But each and every one of you must do as I did. You must rediscover the Cross of Christ in your own heart. Be ready to fight for Him as I have fought. Be ready to suffer for Him as I have suffered. And if you do, you will triumph in the end as I have triumphed."

Sancta Helena, ora pro nobis!